DEAD Sexy

Second Endings #1

Lulu M. Sylvian

GRIFFYN INK

Editing: Full Bloom Editorial

Cover: Laura Medeiros

❀ Formatted with Vellum

For all the muses I've loved before...

Now Hollywood Report: Peter Keith— best known for his teen role in the network sitcom series "Trouble Trouble"— was found dead in his home in Malibu this morning.

Keith's estranged wife discovered his body after she arrived at his home to go over divorce documents.

Coroner's Offices have not made any confirming reports, but Keith's wife has stated that he was taking fentanyl to increase the pain killing effects of an Oxycodone prescription for severe back pain. If true, Keith is another celebrity lost to the opioid crisis plaguing this country. He was fifty-six.

1

I will never forget the details of meeting Peter Keith. The dream was sparkly and shiny. He was *not*. He wore tight, faded jeans and a dark shirt with the sleeves pushed up, and a black leather vest. His straight blond hair parted in the middle and slightly feathered from the front toward the longer, ubiquitous mullet of the early nineteen-nineties in the back. He was clearly not part of the dream. He didn't fit in.

He looked right at me with those big brown eyes. They were full of pain. After I woke up, Peter and those eyes stuck with me all day.

I remembered meeting him so profoundly, I felt obliged to comment the following morning on my social media.

Weird dream with Peter Keith last night, the post read.

Okay, I admit, I feel obliged to comment about most things on social media. I'm not a total narcissist, I'm just a child of the times. While I don't post pictures of every meal I eat, and I may not post daily selfies, the habit of the over-share has been a long time in the making.

Someone commented, *Wasn't he the Trouble Trouble guy?*

I had such a crush on him. Didn't you? I responded to this comment because I did have a little crush on him when I was about five. It didn't last long and then I moved on and fell deeply in love with the color sparkly-purple. It had to be sparkly and purple, or it wasn't true love. To this day, purple is my go-to color.

So, I shared my dream vision with the internet. I'm kind of glad I did. It gives me a date that I can go back, and see and know, I met Peter Keith, TV hottie and teenybopper magazine favorite about six months *after* he died.

When Peter died and all the news stories circulated, I probably commented something like, *"Oh how sad,"* or *"RIP Peter."* I didn't pay much attention beyond that. And then there he was, six months later, in the middle of my dreams, not fitting in.

We were in a smoky bar in the mid-twentieth century. Another dream with Peter, he had been here, in my dreams, every night for at least two weeks. Again, Peter didn't fit in, he never did. It was almost as if the lighting effects on him were not the same lights that illuminated the rest of the dream.

This dream was film noir, black and white, men with big shouldered jackets and fedoras. Peter was in full Kodachrome color, jeans, and that leather vest. He wasn't even obscured by the smoke that hung in the air. He pushed away from a wall he leaned against. I assumed he would walk away as he frequently did after observing everything.

I let the actions of my dream continue, but I pulled myself out and stopped interacting with the dream. "So that's it? You're just going to watch, like this is some kind of a movie? And when the plot doesn't suit you, you just leave? These are my dreams mister, not your cheap entertainment."

He stopped, turned around, and approached me. He looked deep into my eyes, taking my breath away, and then said, "I'll see you later." And then he walked off.

Those were the very first words Peter Keith said to me. I guess that's the moment my relationship, if it could be called a relationship, with Peter began.

I like to think I had my shit together when I met Peter. I survived that gut wrenching year of being twenty-nine, and turning thirty. I had a fantastic place to live with a great roommate, and rent I could afford. I finally had a career-level job as an in-house medical illustrator for the big medical teaching university. And I had the most wonderful boyfriend, who I really was beginning to think was 'the one.' I loved where I lived. I loved my job. I was good. I was not looking for complications.

Complication was spelled P-E-T-E-R-K-E-I-T- H.

"What are you doing, Gilly?" My roommate Mike liked to ask easy, obvious questions. He dumped his groceries on the kitchen counter and came to stand behind the couch where I sat.

"I'm watching a show." I pointed to my laptop set up on the table in front of me. Behind that was the wall of black that was Mike's ridiculously large television. Mike was a TV junky, and frankly, his set up with all the bells and whistles, intimidated me.

"Why aren't you watching it on the TV?"

"I don't want to break it," I confessed.

"C'mon Gil, take notes, I'll set you up. What are you watching anyway?" Mike pushed buttons on remotes. He had a bucket of them, since there really was no such thing as a universal remote for all of those devices.

"That old show *Trouble Trouble*."

"Ooh, with that cute little boy, what was his name?"

"Johnny?"

Mike paused, his hand placed over his heart as if it were going to flutter out of his chest. "Such a hottie. Love me some blond surfer boy. What episode are we on? Are we binge watching? Can we start from the beginning?"

I loved how it went from just me watching, to *we* watching as Mike set the TV up, and got season one, episode one ready for action.

I made popcorn. Mike made margaritas. We watched Peter for six glorious hours.

Mike and I sat next to each other and squealed when Peter jumped down those last three stairs of the set's living-room and waggled his eyebrows. We cringed at how they dressed him. Who thought baggy pants and baggy shirts in neon colors were attractive? Why did they do that to him? In season two they started dressing him in his signature look for the rest of the show, a little more bad-boy in Levi 501s and a leather vest. But the makeup people kind of negated any benefits of the new style by giving Peter a perm. He had a fuzzy blond mullet, it was painful to watch.

Trouble Trouble had been the most popular TV sitcom in the late eighties, early nineties. Peter played Johnny, the insanely cute older brother of twin girls. The plot revolved around the girls and the shenanigans they would cause or get into as identical twins. Johnny was frequently the butt of their jokes, and occasionally their heroic older brother. He was a bit of a dork, otherwise with his good looks, he would have been too perfect.

After that first mini-marathon, Mondays became *Trouble*

Trouble night. We had to limit ourselves to no more than six episodes at a time or we would never go to sleep, or work. That show ran for something like eight years and had two hundred plus episodes.

I became obsessed with Peter. He was in my dreams almost every night and on screen when I was awake. He had been so good looking. He had a chiseled face, a high brow, broad high cheek bones, square jaw tapering to a strong rounded chin. His lips were pleasantly full without being feminine. He had a straight nose that turned up ever so slightly at the end.

In my opinion, his best feature was his eyes. They were big and round and soft, a rich teddy bear brown rimmed with black lashes. I got all fuzzy when I thought about his eyes. He stood just at six feet tall, and had well defined muscles. He kept his silky-straight blond hair a little on the long side. A classic mullet, and then, when he got a little older, the front grew a bit longer, the feathers left as did the mullet. After that, he had kept his hair mostly generic medium long and on the shaggy side.

I retro-actively developed a new crush on him. David, my dream-man, lover, boy-toy, laughed at me about it, and promptly ignored my silliness, as he should. After all, how was a crush on a dead guy going to do any harm to our rock solid relationship?

Dreams with Peter were not the typical mini-movie style of normal dreams. They felt real. I couldn't distinguish them from an actual memory. Had they actually happened? Where was the line between dream and reality?

I sat cross legged on my bed. Peter sat next to me, he braced his feet against the floor, and gripped the edge of my mattress as if was all that kept him from leaping off into space. He was overwhelmingly sad, all slumped into himself. I didn't know what to do for him. Pain rolled off him in tangible waves.

I stroked his back and murmured comforting sounds. I don't know how long we sat like that. I don't remember how we got there, but it had been the same for several nights in a row now. Sometimes, I would be tucked up under blankets, sometimes, I would sit next to him. We would sit, and though I don't remember actually talking, we talked. Peter told me all about his life, and I told him about mine. Tonight was different, he didn't speak.

I leaned against his back, and tried to rub the tension out of his arm. His grip was so hard I was afraid he would rip my bedding. He snatched his arm up and away from me like a cat. I let him, I didn't want to hurt him.

"I don't know what to do for you, Peter." Probably a stupid thing to say, but I didn't know what to do. My heart broke for him.

He shook his head. "It's not fair. It's just not fair."

I didn't exactly know what he was talking about, and yet, I knew he meant having died. When he turned to me, his eyes were rimmed with dark pink. Full of pain and tears.

I adjusted myself on the bed and reached up to guide him down to my lap. His legs stretched out, and hung over the end of my bed. His head rested on my thigh, his breath hot against my skin. With out of focus eyes, he stared into the void.

I stroked his hair, and watched his face. Even in his sadness, he was beautiful, and large. I tried to soothe him until the texture of his shaggy hair made my fingertips go numb. Are men's heads always so big? Why did I think the weirdest things at the most inopportune moments?

I whispered, "I'd help you if I knew what you needed."

He rolled his face into my leg. I could feel his body quake.

I curled over him and held him the best I could. He hurt, and somehow, he found me. I felt like there was a reason for this, and I wanted to help.

I rolled over and woke with a snort. My dream of holding Peter was replaced with the reality of my bedroom in the middle of the night and David's naked shoulder in front of me. I reached up to pet his skin. How different these two men were—one so very real, and one in so much pain.

I closed my eyes to go back to sleep. I had to remember to ask my friend Trina what she thought about tonight's dream with Peter. She would tell me to stop analyzing everything so much and find out what the man wanted. Clearly, he wanted something. I rolled over, safe in the confidence that my best friend would not judge me for thinking I had a pet ghost of some dead actor.

2

I swiped at my eyes, and quietly cussed the allergy gods about how badly they watered. I placed the metal erasing template down on my paper, and gently ran the white hi-polymer eraser over the errant pencil marks. I blinked. Maybe this wasn't allergies, maybe I had eraser crumbs in my eyes.

I left my drawing table in my super-sized double cube—perks of being the only departmental illustrator—and went to the restroom. Once out in the hallway, my waterfall leakage calmed down. Not one to waste a trip, I made use of the destination. When I finished, I washed up and decided to wash my face. Allergens and stray eraser bits could whirl away down the sink.

I felt better until I slid back onto my stool, and damn if my eyes didn't start leaking again. I needed a distraction to keep me from thinking about my watery eyes. This illustration was not claiming all of my attention.

"Okay line, you need to be a happy little representation of a virus." I found that talking to the illustrations did actually make them behave. Sometimes, I would even narrate the drawing process like I was on a TV painting show.

My mother used to paint.

"Oh, yeah?"

Yeah. I would sit and watch her.

"You didn't want to paint?"

I wasn't old enough, I don't think. I would play with my Matchbox cars and she would stand in the light and paint flower vases set up on our kitchen table.

I pictured Peter sitting behind me. In my head, he wore a pink striped polo and played with pens while we carried on a perfectly mundane conversation. This was exactly the kind of side distraction my brain needed so than my fingers could turn pencil lead into viral receptors.

I didn't pay much attention to him being there, because I honestly thought nothing of it. A nice little pretend conversation with my imaginary friend—that wasn't exactly not normal for me. Why wouldn't my recurring dreams turn into a day dream? He hung out and we chatted for most of the afternoon.

He showed up again the next day. Same place, in my cubicle while I worked. This time, my eyes only watered a bit. Really, no more than if I had yawned really hard, not the down pour of the day before.

I was very much focused on the particular anatomy of a specific viral receptor structure in cellular walls. I needed to get this right, the article I read had all of my attention. So, when he spoke, I dropped the medical journal I held and looked for him. I could have sworn he was there. Of course, I couldn't see anything. I tried to go back to my research when I heard him chuckle.

"All right," I said out loud as I turned and got up from my desk. "Who's that?" I looked out of my cube to see if anyone walked past, figuring that must have been what I heard. I popped my head over the wall to peak at my cubicle neighbor, but she wore headphones and focused on her computer pretty intently.

Now, the day before my mind had really been wandering all over the place, and I had probably already been talking to myself. So, I would have assumed that's all my Peter conversation had really been, voices in my head entertaining me.

I'm right here, Gillian.

I heard him as clearly as if he stood right next to me. But there was no one there. I turned around slowly, and as my gaze passed where he sat and he went just out of my range of vision, my brain picked him up. I spun back around, expecting to see him there. Well, not Peter specifically, but someone.

You didn't mind yesterday, what's up today?

"Yesterday, I was talking to myself," I hissed. "This isn't real."

Close your eyes, and see.

"That makes no sense," I whispered. I was very aware that I was talking to myself all of a sudden, and very self-conscious about it.

Use your brain, not your eyes, he explained.

I closed my eyes and turned back toward where I thought he sat. There he was, sitting in the chair at the drawing table. I opened my eyes, there was no one there. I fumbled to find my desk chair. I was going to fall down. I wanted to land in the chair and not on my ass on the floor. I stared into the empty space. "How?"

Same as yesterday, he said with a shrug.

"But, you're real."

I was real yesterday.

"No, yesterday was my imagination. This is just my imagination. Maybe I need to eat something."

Gil, this is the same as yesterday. Sorry, not your imagination. His spoke in calm, soothing tones.

"Oh my God, oh my God, oh my God." I covered my face with my hands. This was too much. I manifested my day dreams. I took a deep cleansing breath.

"Ok, so you're here. You're actually here?" I asked. I started whispering, very much aware that I was going nuts.

Yeah, I'm here. Even though the conversation took place in my head, it really did sound like he occupied the same space with me.

Why are you here, Peter? The dreams, that's actually you and not just me dreaming is it? I asked in my head.

Nope, that's me too. Since I've been able to get into your dreams, I decided to try this and it worked, he explained.

Okay, so, wow. I don't know what to say. I really was stymied. The previous day, I chatted on and on, but this time, I was at a complete loss.

Why don't you tell me what you're doing? Yesterday it was obvious you were drawing, and you described everything as you went. Today, you're reading magazines.

I couldn't believe he actually took interest in what I was doing. I think it was a ploy to get me to calm down and keep talking.

"I'm researching my next illustration. It needs to show how viruses can plug into cell walls." I gestured with my hands, trying to mimic the action that would happen when receptors engaged.

That sounds like you need to focus, I'll come back. He seemed very understanding.

"Thanks, I do need to focus on this," I said.

He nodded in understanding, and was gone. I wasn't

fully convinced that I hadn't had a mental break, and that I wasn't talking to my new imaginary friend. *Peter?* I first asked in my head, and then out loud, "Peter? Peter?"

I tentatively looked around. I couldn't "see" him. I needed to take a break from work before I mentally snapped, if I hadn't already. I went to the restroom to splash cool water on my face. It took a few times of rinsing before I felt human again. Staring at myself in the mirror didn't help.

Is that what a crazy person looks like? I mean, there are always comments floating around about how crazy redheads are, and with my freckles, blue eyes, and bright orange hair, they don't get much more redheaded than me. Back in my cube, I pretended to work. Regaining my focus on the research took some time, but I was finally able to get my energy back aligned to the task at hand. I could not shake the thought that Peter was real and not simply in my head.

I got used to his presence pretty fast. Within a week, Peter pretty much hung out with me constantly, either at home or at work. Every time he showed up, I would leak a little. The eyes would fill up. A few blinks was all it took to calm things down.

The biggest difference between daytime Peter and dream-time Peter was a lack of sensory input. When he visited during the day, I couldn't hear his movements, something I fully experienced in dreams. Since I couldn't hear him, he really could sneak up on me. I think he actually enjoyed that. I tended to jump. I was being spooked by a ghost. Ironic or expected?

The problem with Peter was he could control how my brain saw him, and he was flirty. There was a comfort level hanging out with middle-aged Peter that I didn't have when he decided to show up looking younger. Older Peter was calm, and didn't interfere. I could focus and work; I could banter the flirt right back into his court. I tended to get giggly and stupid when he showed up looking like Johnny from *Trouble Trouble*. He got a little flirty and I went full fan girl on him. My five-year-old's crush would slam right back into me and I would constantly blush, and stammer, and be generally stupid.

You're crying.

"Shut up." I focused on the onions in front of me and tried to ignore the fact that when I closed my eyes, Peter was distractingly gorgeous. His skin was taut, and there was something about his neck, and that chin. He had never shown up quite this hot before.

Not looking my best, I was in the middle of my food prep for the week. That meant being dressed for chores and involved chopping onions and peppers, making a big pot of rice, and prepping a few crock-pot meals. Crock-pot meals were in the freezer, the rice was on the stove, and the onions were in front of me.

I still needed to hard boil a bunch of eggs. The kitchen in Mike's condo is long and narrow with appliances on one side, and a long island counter with bar stools on the other. I worked at the counter.

I already had one onion chopped and stored in a mason jar, the rest lined up in front of me waiting their turn. Peter sat on one of the bar stools on the opposite side of the island and leaned over watching me chop. The first onion had already started me crying, then Peter showed up, and I leaked even more.

In typical early twenties male fashion, Peter decided my leaking was fodder for picking on me. He had shown up a la Johnny from the show with his silky blond mullet and stone washed jeans. I was defenseless against him. I honestly knew why I was defenseless, even with the dated clothes and bad hair, he was beyond cute, straight into dead sexy, and I went giddy.

You have a cute little nose.

A blush burned my cheeks.

You're blushing.

"Shut up." I blushed harder. I know I turned an even brighter shade of red, and that it ran down my cheeks onto my chest, and probably all the way to my toes. I put the knife down in exasperation.

He leaned farther over the counter and tried to look down my shirt. *You're blushing as far down as I can see.* He laughed.

I clasped my hand to my chest, plastering the V-neck to my skin so there was no gap to look down.

He tried to bop me on the nose. I could almost see him while my focus was on the chopping in front of me. The tears in my eyes welled up again. Interesting, I leaked if he touched me.

So, Gillian, Gilly, Gil. Is your last name really Denver?

Yes, like the city in Colorado. I answered in my head, conscious that Mike might come home at any time and see me talking to thin air. I tried to refocus on the onion. I wanted the vegetable in thin half circle cuts, not my fingers.

I was thinking more like that actor Bob Denver.

Why? No relation that I'm aware of. Or is everything with you somehow connected to TV and Hollywood? I asked.

Gil, like Gilligan, as in Gilligan's Island. Bob Denver played Gilligan, and your last name is Denver and your name is pronounced Gillian like Gilligan. He cocked his head to the side regarding me.

I can't say that I've ever had that connection made before. That was a blatant lie. I had. As a kid more than enough people called me Gilligan. It was not a nick name I was particularly fond of, it was a close second to being called Red. If I knew you and I liked you, I'd accept being called Red. Random people calling me Red, or Gilligan, irked me. Other nicknames that annoyed me included Wendy, Pippy, Carrot Top, and Pumpkin Head. I never got the cool redhead nicknames like Pepper or Ginger or Rusty.

Gilligan, he bopped me on the nose again. My eyes were closed so I almost actually 'saw' the action this time.

I wanted to glare at him, give him my weary, why-are-you-torturing-me-look. I couldn't glare, because I couldn't see him. I couldn't glare, because I was blushing like a stop sign. I pointed my face at him, so I could see him in my brain. He smirked at me.

Cut it out with the nose bops. You keep making me tear up.

That's the onions, Gilligan.

Really, you're gonna call me that now? Pete. I emphasized the shortened variation of his name. David hated being called Dave. I thought the nick-name might annoy Peter. It didn't.

Pete works for me. What would you rather I call you? Red?

I glared into the empty space where he sat. How did he know? He was doing that on purpose. Maybe during one of our previous conversations I admitted to not liking being called Red. Or maybe he had been around enough redheads to gauge that response. Either way, as he toyed with me, I did my best to shoot daggers from my mental eyes.

Ok not Red, he said in defeat.

My focus returned to processing my onions. The timer on the stove beeped, and I grabbed a fork to fluff the rice. Once cooled, I would transfer the rice into a refrigerator container. The onions were almost done. Once the eggs were boiled, my weekly food prep would be complete.

I guess you can call me Gilligan, just not Red. Please not Red, I pleaded, whining. I couldn't begin to describe how much I hated being called Red. *Too many bad memories. I'm serious, okay Peter? Not Red.* I felt the joy leave me thinking about the hell of being called Red as a kid.

His tone was sober as he confirmed, *not Red.*

Peter continued to hang out with me as I finished chopping. I enjoyed my time with him, but the back of my mind tickled with the all mighty "why." Why was Peter hanging out with me? Did he need something from me? Why me?

When it was time to move on to my next get-ready-for-the-week chore he abandoned me. I guess folding laundry and watching TV were not as entertaining as watching me chop onions. Too bad, he missed being able to comment on my underwear.

3

M y best friend, Trina, and her precocious toddler, Sophie, were already making headway into a basket of fries and a bowl of ketchup. A tall iced coke waited for me. I plopped myself into the booth and dropped the stack of notebooks I brought.

"What's all that?" Trina asked.

I pushed one of the spiral notebooks toward her, opened it. Tapping at the page I said, "Read."

Trina squinted at me, but asked no questions. She began reading.

I bounced on my hands and watched. My gaze would jump from her face to the page, then back to her face. She read five pages of my chicken scratch handwriting before she looked up.

"This is good, Gil. When did you decide to start writing?"

I waggled a finger at the notebook. "Keep reading, it's about to get hot. At least, I think it's hot."

Trina returned to the notebook. Her eyes bugged out a bit when she got to the part I wanted her to read. I needed to know if the sex scene I put down was steamy or too much like a wet-dream fantasy of mine.

She looked up. "This is Peter isn't it?" She swiveled the notebook back at me and tapped at a sketch of a superhero quality man with broad shoulders, a modern take on that nineteen-eighty's mullet. Underneath, I had a close up of his eyes.

"Uh huh." I nodded.

As my one true bestie, I confided in Trina about my dreams with Peter. As an energy worker and crystal healer, she accepted my stories and helped me to figure out how to deal with Peter. She was the metaphysical-yin to my scientific-yang.

"I might need a cold shower after this," she said returning to the story I had written. "I guess it's a good thing I can't see him for real, 'cause I might blush." She closed the notebook and pushed it back to me. "That's hot. Where did that come from?"

I was still bouncing, excited to finally be able to share it with her.

"I know what Peter wants. This just started pouring out of my fingers. I know he's somehow feeding it to me. It feels like I can't write it fast enough," I explained, or thought I had explained.

"What does Peter want, Gil?"

I turned to the back of one of the notebooks and gave Sophie a pen so she could scribble while we talked. Trina pulled out another pen for Sophie. She had two colors to draw with, and was completely occupied.

"He wants a do-over. He feels like he really messed things up the last five to ten years or so of his life. So," I paused dramatically, "with his help, I'm recreating his life from the point he thinks things went wrong. I'm going to write a book. I know so much about what needs to happen. Things Peter has said are coming together, and I'm going to switch it around. He once told me he fell in love with the wrong woman, and he made some bad choices as an actor. So, he's going to become Johnny Urban. Johnny Urban successfully makes the transition from child protégé pop-star to action-hero. The story is after that point, but he's got that history as a singer so I can have him serenade the girl.

"I'm writing it the way Peter wishes things had happened. Like, instead of turning down a smaller role in a bigger movie to take a bigger role in a smaller movie, he's going to take that smaller role. Johnny Urban will own that part and character so completely, everyone notices, and bigger parts start coming in. In the middle of this career surge, he's surrounded by beautiful starlets, and dates a few of them but never anything serious.

"He meets this girl. Completely not the Hollywood type. And he keeps seeing her day after day at this bus stop. She is the most beautiful thing he has ever seen. I'm not sure if she's heard of him or not. I kind of like the idea that she's not a big movie watcher, so doesn't know who he is. Or maybe she does know and isn't a fan-girl type. Anyway, they talk, and they become friends. Eventually, they start dating, blah, blah, blah, yadda, yadda, yadda. What do you think so far?" I was excited, and desperate for some feedback.

"I think you need to breathe!"

I guess I had been going on non-stop. I felt charged. I knew what Peter needed, and with his help, this was really easy. I had never considered myself much of a writer before, but the words were rushing out of my fingers. I needed to practice my typing skills—I wrote by hand faster than I could type. At some point, I would have to transcribe all those pages.

So far, I had filled one and a half spiral notebooks with the story of Johnny Urban and Michelle Cole. I knew exactly what needed to happen. Johnny Urban would meet and fall in love with a woman not in the film industry, and not a fan. She was going to be interested in him because he made her laugh, and not because of his fame.

He would still be injured, but instead of ignoring physical therapy and getting back into acting too soon, he would actually take time off to properly recover, and start a family. I knew that was one of Peter's big regrets, he didn't have any kids. He had told me it was something he really missed about *Trouble Trouble*, the cast felt more like a family than a group of people who worked together.

He wasn't from a big family, and only had one brother. They had been close as kids, but grew apart as adults. By writing it out, I could help Peter repair that relationship, give him a bigger, closer family. Create, in fiction, a world he would have been happier in.

"Well, I can't wait to read more. What genre are you going for? Chick lit? Romance? General fiction? Erotica?" Trina laughed at that last one.

"I think it will be romance, a nice contemporary romance. That way I can focus on the relationships that seem to be the most important. I don't think I could write it if it was suspense and action heavy, or even a mystery. I have no idea if I'm any good at weaving all those pieces together that you get in really thick fiction. You know, the kinds with lots of characters and they each have a storyline that somehow feeds into to bigger picture. I don't know if I can do that bigger-picture fiction, so far this smaller focused storyline with a few key relationships seems to be working."

My lunch arrived and I stabbed the salad I ordered. Why was I trying to be healthy today? "I have all these little ideas and scenes in my head. I have to change his look, I don't want anyone reading it to instantly think of Peter Keith, but I still need it to be Peter. I can't picture him with dark hair in my mind, so maybe I'll make him taller and give him blue eyes. But, he needs to keep the blond hair."

"Maybe they'll think it's the character from *Trouble Trouble* instead."

"Yeah, I did use the name Johnny. I needed for there to be some connection. I almost considered using his name, Peter, or even Keith. I'm writing this for him really, but he wants other people to see it. That means I really am writing this to see if I can get something published."

"Is that something you want to do? Write his story and become a published author?"

"Why not? I have all these other stories in my head. Things I mostly thought I would someday either animate or create a graphic novel of. Why not try my hand at just writing? It could be fun."

Trina nodded as she chewed. "So, what do you get out of it? You're helping Peter, what is he going to do for you? Or is he just a muse?"

"He promised that he would help me get one of my ideas written out. I'll help him with his story, and then he'll help me with mine."

"And what's this idea of yours?"

I had been holding this idea in my head for so long, it was a relief to finally tell someone and not have them think I was a random weirdo. Trina knew I was a creative weirdo. My hands flew as I spoke. "I've wanted to do a graphic novel. Science fiction, a worlds collide, Martian invasion type of thing. Okay, so this one time, when my hair was longer, and, okay don't get grossed out on me. When I wash my hair and it pulls out, I would get the hair off my hands by putting it on the shower wall. Sometimes, I would forget to clean it off afterwards, and it would dry stuck to the shower wall. I started to notice shapes in the strands of hair. What if there were hidden messages in the hair?

"So then, I thought what if I meshed the secret messages in the hair with the invading aliens? I think it would be cool. It would have to include psychics and talking bugs. It never really went anywhere. Peter said it was an interesting idea and he would help me do something with it." I was beyond animated describing this surreal, dreamlike idea to her.

Trina was my opposite. Calm and collected to my frantic enthusiasm. "That is an interesting idea. And you said he's willing to help you develop it?"

I nodded with fervor.

"Seems like a fair enough trade." Trina nodded. After a few bites of food, she asked, "How are things with David?"

David and I were in that comfortable with each other phase of the relationship, spending weekends together, and one or two mid-week dates. Then she told me all about her latest fiasco with the mother-in-law. I listened and lived the family life vicariously through Trina, taking mental notes on how to deal with my future mother-in-law. I liked David's mother. I think we would get along just fine in a mother-daughter role. David just needed to catch up.

4

When I got home after work, I was eager to get back to writing. I had already spent every non-work minute doing so. Peter's story was taking on a life of its own, and I wanted to see where it went next.

Mike sat watching TV when I came in the back door. I tossed my keys onto the counter and stared at the television before making my way up to my room.

"Hey Mike," I said as I began climbing the stairs. "You watching football again?" I didn't understand the game, and Mike seemed to not care about any specific team or the scores, yet he watched it a lot.

"No, I'm watching the locker room. It's so homoerotic."

I laughed. "It's only homoerotic because you're a homo and you find it erotic."

"You are not wrong there, girlfriend. Just look at all that beef cake." Mike pointed at the screen. I tried to see it from his point of view. Big sweaty men wandering around in assorted stages of being geared up and undressing. Okay, that caught my attention. Thighs, tight butts, and, ooh, one of them walked passed the camera in just a towel. Dang, the man was built like a comic book hero, all muscles, shaped like an inverted triangle, and with that Adonis belt V.

I sat down, pulled in by the skin show. "I think I may have under estimated this sport."

"And you always thought I was nuts for watching football."

"Is this why you watch soccer too?"

He answered with a, "Hmmm-mmm. Soccer butts are amazing."

I was strangely drawn in by all the male anatomy, but my writing demanded attention. I got up. "Well, have fun, and no drooling on the upholstery. Hey, should I make a lot of noise if I come back down? Ya know, in case you decide you need some private time to take yourself to the next level here?"

Mike threw some serious shade at me. The man perfected the disapproving side glance, laser eye. "Don't be crass."

I laughed then started to run up the stairs.

"Wait, Gilly, I'm glad you're home. I have to ask you something." Mike had swiveled around to look at me. He sounded pretty serious, so I changed direction and plopped back down on the couch next to him.

"S'up?" I hadn't noticed any quaver to his voice, but he actually looked concerned, his dark almond shaped eyes wide. Suddenly, he looked like a frail Korean boy-band singer, pretty and over dramatic.

"Mike, you okay?"

His appearance took on a whole new pallor as he thought about what he needed to say. Crap, I hope he wasn't evicting me. I paid my rent on time. He took a long moment, centering himself. He held his hand to his chest, long narrow fingers resting below his collar bone.

"I've been seeing something the past few days on and off, and today, it freaked me out." He took in a deep breath.

I squinted at him, tilting my head in question.

"Gilly, I think we have a ghost."

I sat back and bit my thumbnail.

"You can see him too?" I whispered.

Mike gasped, covered his mouth as he pulled back from me. "I thought I was crazy, but I swear I keep seeing a big cat on the stairs. You've seen it?"

I sighed, relaxing a bit. I thought he was talking about Peter. Yes we had a cat ghost. I was so used to it walking in and out of my life, I really hadn't thought about it. Poor Mike, the cat really was freaking him out.

"Yeah," I drawled out the word, trying to figure out how to tell Mike he really was seeing a cat, and hoping he didn't freak and kick me out. "I'm sorry I didn't warn you about him. He's a friendly, if that helps."

"Warn me? You moved in with a pet ghost? I might need a security deposit for that," Mike giggled. Good, he was relaxing.

"I've had this spirit cat following me around off and on for the past ten years or so," I began explaining. "He, I think it's a he, showed up in college. He usually just slinks around the hallways. He's shown up at almost every place I've lived. I've even gotten into the habit of telling him when I'm getting ready to move so he knows to follow."

"And you didn't think to share this with me?"

I snorted. "Right, and just how does one announce when looking for a place to live they are bringing their ghost animals with them?"

"Good point," he conceded.

"Honestly Mike, you're the first roommate I've had who has ever seen him. He must like you."

"What does it mean, why is he here?" Mike was searching for some deeper meaning to the cat.

I shrugged. "I honestly don't know. He never seems to precede some kind of danger or stress. So, he's not a harbinger of any kind. He just shows up and makes me wonder why there's a cat there. I think he's comfortable here."

"So, what you're saying is he's a nice ghost kitty?"

I nodded. I thought about telling him about Peter—then again maybe not. He freaked out over the cat. When people don't see spirits regularly, I understand how it would freak them out. Heck, Mr. Cat caught me off guard more than once and spooked me a few times. I decided I wouldn't tell Mike about the other cat—the Thing.

I had two cats that would visit me, occasionally. They would wander around for a while, then curl up in a window and "sleep" mostly. I guess if it looks like ghost cat is sleeping, that is what ghost cat is doing.

Now, the Thing could be positively freaky. The Thing was big and grey, and it swam. I wasn't really sure what it was. Dolphin? Shark? Matinee? Kraken? When the Thing would swim past and brush up against me, it made everything go ice cold and I could feel the water ebb and flow around me. In all fairness, I hadn't seen the Thing in several years, unlike the cats who I saw last month.

I decided to not tell Mike about the Thing. Cats were one issue—the Thing was a whole different level of ghostly weirdness.

I had started back up the stairs before I remembered to ask, "Mike, when you saw the cat, what color was he?"

"What do you mean what color?"

"I was just wondering if it was the big black one or the ginger tabby." I ran up the stairs.

Mike called after me, "There are two of them?"

"Yep, we've got two ghost cats." I ducked into my room. I was trying not to laugh. I had whammied Mike there at the end.

Peter sat on my side chair chuckling

"Did you hear all that?" I asked out loud before switching to head talk. I didn't need Mike finding out about the full grown human ghost too.

Yeah. I've never seen these cats of yours, Peter confessed.

Can't you see other ghosts? I asked, curious if there were more spirits or entities out there that I couldn't recognize.

Not that I can tell. But then again, I can't talk to people either. I can get inside their heads, and I can hear them if they are projecting their thoughts. But you seem to be the only one who can hear and see me.

As interesting as talking ghost capability skill sets was, I wanted to show Peter what I had worked on. I kicked off my shoes and took the stack of notebooks into the center of my bed. Peter joined me. I opened the most recent one—I had half-way filled my third spiral notebook.

I wrote about when Peter, I mean Johnny, first started acting. It was a tension filled scene between him and his music manager. As an aging pop sensation, Johnny struggled to stay relevant. His original fan base was older, he wanted to age up his art to maintain their fan dollars. His bubble gum sappy love songs were no longer on trend. Musicals were struggling to make a comeback. One of those would be a perfect transition into film for the singer. Instead of admitting that he didn't know how to take Johnny into film, his manager sabotaged his shot at a leading role.

I like it. Brings in some tension so that the love story will be a welcome sigh of relief.

I flipped forward to another scenario I had thought

about. Since vampires and werewolves were so popular, I thought it would be awesome to make Johnny one.

Look, I pointed to a passage I written. *Here, if Johnny is a vampire, we can explain how or why he's injured.*

You want the injury for me to become a vampire? Peter sighed heavily. *Then I can't go on to have children.* He shook his head discontentedly at me, like I was a dumb kid that should know better.

Okay, no vampires. I wanted him to be a vampire. I had also started developing some ideas in case Peter hadn't liked the vampire concept. I wasn't going to present them to him until they were more fully formed.

So, then what needs to happen here? I tapped the writing with my pencil. Talking to Peter felt like I actively and purposefully thought through a concept with myself. Even while working closely together like this, I had doubts to his reality. After all, if I talked to pencil lines as I drew, why not talk to characters as I wrote?

The injury needs to be bigger. I shook it off like it wasn't a big deal. That was a mistake.

I scribbled, trying to get the words out as fast as I could.

Johnny leapt. This was an easy jump. The camera angle would make the jump appear at least twice as far as it really was. He had already practiced it several times. The leap leaving the gondola was well-choreographed. It should have been a simple two quick steps then jump.

Something went wrong as he pushed away from the gondola. His feet hadn't taken the right stepping sequence. He was off. His arm smashed down on the corner of the bricks. Sharp white pain shot up his arm and down into his fingers. His palm should have made contact first but his wrist caught the edge making his hand go numb. He scrambled to grab hold with his other hand. His grip wasn't enough to hold him. This should have been a simple stunt, he thought as he dropped. The fall wasn't from a great height, but it wasn't anticipated. He wasn't in position to catch himself properly.

"Fuck!" Johnny bit out as he landed, his ankle buckled, and then his leg twisted and collapsed under him. The leg was painful, but it was the unexpected jar to the back that knocked the breath out of Johnny, causing him to drop to the ground and rock back and forth in pain.

I swung the notebook around for Peter to see. He was quiet as he regarded what I had written. I wanted to see him with my eyes, but I couldn't, so I closed my eyes and looked with my brain.

His eyes were large and round when he looked up at me. *That's exactly how it happened, how?* He shook his head.

This is what you're putting into my head as you talk. Your words are describing events but I'm also tapped into your memories somehow. You're giving this all to me, the more you talk, the more I know about your life. So, I opened my eyes staring into the empty space where his body wasn't, before closing them again in order to see him, *does it work?*

Peter nodded.

I continued to write. Making the injury and Johnny's reaction to it bigger than what Peter had gone through. Peter had fallen. He had not caught himself properly on a leap from a hanging gondola to a brick wall. The drop had only been about twelve feet, but unprepared, it was enough to really mess up his back.

Peter's injuries had consisted of a wrist abrasion, a twisted ankle, and what was discovered much later, fractured vertebrae. Not taking his injury seriously and not going to a doctor right away, put him on the wrong path— away from proper healing and recovering. Johnny had a similar fall, but I wrote that he broke his leg and his back.

The broken leg put him in a position where he had to get taken to a hospital and be properly x-rayed.

Peter, trying to be a tough guy in real life, did himself a disservice. I made Johnny more humble in a way Peter realized he should have been in his life.

We kept working like this for a few more hours. I wanted to make Johnny a werewolf after Peter said no to the vampire idea. He did not like that idea either. I tried a variety of shape shifter animals out on him, thinking that maybe if I tapped into the right spirit animal for him he would acquiesce. I thought he would make a beautiful were-tiger.

We managed to fill the rest of that notebook before my phone started pinging with a bunch of text messages.

I grabbed it. "It's David. Goodnight, Peter."

Goodnight. He chuckled. He knew what I was getting ready to do. Peter didn't fade away, one moment he was there, the next he was just gone. I cleared the notebooks off my bed, and snuggled back into the pillows. It was time for flirty, dirty sexting with my boyfriend.

5

The more I wrote, the easier it got. I seemed to instinctively know what had happened in Peter's life. I knew exactly how to change it up for Johnny's version of the story. I wrote almost every night. I had no idea what I was doing, just writing. Without knowing how many words made a book, I started estimating word counts in some of my favorite romance novels. They all seemed to have around a hundred-thousand words. That's an intimidating number. My best guess was I had about ten thousand words per spiral notebook. I was going to need to fill at least ten notebooks to be even close to my needed goal.

My typing skills were something to be afraid of. I was a speed pecker. I typed with no more than four fingers total, on both hands. I was clueless how to even begin learning how to touch type. Getting the handwritten words into the computer was a daunting task I was not yet ready to face.

Writing had become an addiction. I thought about it even while at work. My days filled up fast, and I had no free time. I spent it all writing. If I wasn't careful I was going to burn out. The only down time I seemed to allow myself anymore was watching *Trouble Trouble* with Mike. During *Trouble Trouble* I could turn off and enjoy watching Peter. However, my mind kept cranking out story content whenever I tried watching other shows.

I started thinking in narrative. My actions were mentally noted in third person—*Gillian noted with some concern the light at the bottom of the stairwell flickered. It reminded her of too many horror movies. She thought if she went down one more level of stairs there would be a jump scare waiting for her. This was work, which was scary enough. Would the jump scare be zombies, a crazed killer, or merely Holly, the office manager walking through the door at the exact same moment Gil starts to pull it open?*

I constantly looked for better adjectives and verbs. I stopped speaking and began enunciating, growling, or whispering. My speaking vocabulary slowly began to evolve as well. I no longer said 'awesome' about everything that I found mildly interesting or cool. Interesting became intriguing, captivating, or something would pique my curiosity. Cool became more definitive as delightful, all right, or my new favorite—hunky-dory. The thesaurus became my new best friend.

I continued my weekly lunches with Trina, whenever she didn't cancel on me, but I begged off lunches with my office manager Holly in order to write. I focused so much on Peter I was afraid my relationship with David would begin to suffer. I had already started letting my friendship with Holly slip because I had a new and exciting friend. I really didn't want to mess up with David.

David and I were destined to be together after we met at a Halloween party a few years back—the fates doing their finest work. My roommate "dragged" me out for the evening to a fabulous party full of pretty men. David came dressed as the Doctor from that popular British show. He wore a pinstriped suit with a dark blue shirt and an ugly tie. He actually looks like the actor with short brown hair, a broad brow, sharp cheekbones, a straight sharp nose, a sharp chin, and thin lips. Even his name was David. I thought he was so cute, all tall and skinny and geeky—and straight. Just my type.

It had to be fate because I dressed up like a different character from the same show. My hair was long then, so it was perfect. I wore a short black skirt, a white shirt, and a black vest that I had painted "POLICE" in white across the back. I wore it with a little checkered black and white scarf around my neck. Only, I was a bit more extreme than the TV character, since I really was in drag-queen level make up, and my hair was teased about a mile high.

As soon as we met, I didn't leave his side. We got along like a house on fire. And when he kissed me the first time, I felt it tingle in my toes. I was instantly smitten, and it seemed like he was too. Toward the end of the night, when he held out his hand and said, "Allons-y,"—I went.

David stopped taking me out as much during the week, and until Peter made some snide comment questioning my loyalties, I hadn't even really noticed. I reacted negatively to that. Peter was my imaginary friend, not my boyfriend, and not someone I was going to cheat on my boyfriend with— not that I even could if I had wanted to, with him being non-corporeal and mostly made up. I was in a committed relationship—one that I hoped would become even more committed in the future.

As soon as Peter pointed that out, I immediately texted David. We needed to put in some quality relationship time.

"Hey I feel like I haven't seen you in forever." I texted.

"Who are you again?" David replied.

"Ha ha, funny. Seriously I miss u. Can u talk?"

"Can't talk, but can text. What's up?"

I sighed, what was up? I wasn't seeing David as much as usual. How did I tell him without sounding clingy? Humor and demands would be my approach.

"You need to feed me and show me your naked body soon."

"Lol Gil, sure. When?"

"You tell me."

"How about sushi and naked on Thursday?"

Sushi? Who the hell did David think he was talking to? I was not a sushi fan. I was so not a sushi fan. I tried it once, my gag reflex kicked in and with cosmic bad timing, I threw up all over the table, in front of everybody, in the middle of a crowded restaurant. Not my finest hour. Between the texture and being humiliated by raw fish, there was no way I would ever try it again. David knew this. Clearly, he wasn't thinking, or I was texting a different David.

"You realize you are texting me right?"

"Yes, Gil.

"Sushi? WTF?"

"Sorry, Gil, distracted. Thursday I'll pick you up at work. We can decide on food later ok? I need to focus now."

"Ok, can't wait."

David needed to focus. He regularly attended Meet-up groups and other presentations for work. I figured that was what I distracted him from.

I turned to Peter. "Are you happy now? I have a date on Thursday."

It's not about my happiness, Gilligan, it's about yours. He sounded smug.

∾

"Oh, yum. " I gushed enthusiastically as the waiter delivered dinner. Lamb kabobs over saffron rice.

"You're drooling," David said as if he had never seen me around food before.

I had already eaten slightly more than half of the stuffed grape leaf appetizers. The savory warm smells tickled my nose and teased my stomach.

"Thank you." I smiled up at our waiter, and tucked in with a large scoop of rice right into my open maw. "Have you met me?" I asked around a mouth full of food. I had the metabolism of a teenage boy on meth. Empty calories and I were good friends, I just wished at some point they would convert to boob fat.

I stared at David like I was looking at him for the first time. He was so cute, but something was different. He gave me a pleasant smile and tucked his napkin back onto his lap. He ate with precise, fussy movements. Typically, David would be "that guy" who held onto the skewer and bit straight into the meat before sliding the chunks of grilled goodness onto the plate. Not that David was tacky, he was fun. Maybe obnoxiously fun at times, but fussy and precise table manners were something he would reserve for dinner around my grandmother.

Our morning schedules and whose place was closer determined where we ended up. Not so secretly, I preferred my bigger bed and nicer bathroom. I picked the kabob place because it was closer to my bedroom.

About a year after I moved in with Mike, after being in this job for six months, I got sick and tired of sleeping in a single bed. I'm an adult, and I wanted an adult bed, one big enough to share. The universe was never going to take me seriously, wanting a relationship if I slept in a single bed. As soon as I determined I could afford a new mattress, I waited for the next big sale. Not only did I score a king sized bed for the cost of a double, they paid the sales tax, delivered the mattresses, and hauled off my old one. I loaded up my new bed with pillows and fluffy blankets. My bedroom looked like a mermaid's boudoir all in sea greens and blues, and full of eclectic treasures.

Big comfy bed and the best lover I ever had, it was a good night. I think part of why David was so good was because we had been able to develop as a couple. Having been together for a while, we knew each other's on-buttons quite well. He may have been skinny, and a little soft in the middle, but he had good arms and legs. His chest wasn't roped with heavy pectoral muscles. I didn't care. I loved him, and I would have even with a little more pudge and man-boob action. I loved his brain, his sense of humor, and his wicked grin. I didn't love him because of his looks, but that certainly helped the initial attraction.

I particularly loved what David did to me. Warm skin on skin. A bite here, a nip there. A suck, a lick. It always felt so good. That night wasn't any different. I could taste the beer he had with dinner on his tongue as we kissed. Everything tingled as we twined together. David did his thing, I enjoyed it completely, closing my eyes and losing myself to the sensations. For some reason, I opened my brain and looked straight into Peter's eyes.

Peter's ability to appear and disappear at random could be inconvenient. Inconvenient is the nice word I'm going to use, and not the string of curse words he inspired. I wondered if Peter was checking up on me because David had cancelled on me for the week before, and I hadn't seen him all weekend. Peter was used to me being available, and this time had picked a really inopportune moment to pop in.

My eyes flew open. Nothing. I closed them again. Peter was right there, leaning on my dresser, in all his naked glory. He looked like he wanted to participate, more than turned on by what David and I were doing.

Peter appeared in top physical shape. Don't get me wrong, I loved David but he was never going to be an underwear model or turn heads on a beach. Peter, on the other hand, had a model's physique. His chest was broad and well-defined, his shoulders and arms bulged with muscles. His abs rippled with ridges like a washboard. He wasn't overly big like a body builder, just extremely well defined.

And I could see all of it. I do mean—all of it. I had an uninterrupted view of his torso from the top of his head to below his knees. He was well proportioned, if not a bit bigger than I would have guessed. Perfectly thick and long. He took care by hand, what David and I were able to take care of together. I found it to be incredibly sexy and it heightened everything for me.

I watched Peter, I felt David. Peter's hand matched the pace David's hips set. As I reached my pinnacle, I refocused on David. We peaked in quick succession. Everything felt loose and all my muscles turned to liquid. David went off to clean up, I limply turned to Peter. The smile he gave me was wicked and sexy. I should have thought then that I might be in trouble, especially when I realized I really wanted to feel Peter on my body. I know I'd had wonderful sex with the man I loved, but my body wanted more, and Peter appeared ready and willing, too bad he couldn't actually touch me.

I pointed at him and said, "You really should not be here right now. You need to leave."

Peter nodded and faded. I was too limp to be angry. David felt so warm and comfortable when he returned to bed and curled up against me.

The next morning, when I had regained my senses, I became enraged. How dare Peter show up and indiscreetly hang about watching David and I bumping uglies? I needed to have a talk with Peter about that. David and I were not there to put on a sex show. That was for private personal enjoyment only. Thank you very much.

I really wished that ghosts could get text messages. I had no way of communicating with Peter, he always came to me. I couldn't call him, I couldn't text him, and I couldn't email him. I couldn't will him into existence. It was incredibly unfair. I wanted to talk to him about personal boundaries while it was all fresh in my mind. But I had to wait, and hope I remembered what it was I needed to discuss with him, and not get distracted by developments in the book with Johnny and Michelle.

Trina needed a new dress for a family wedding. She was tired of wearing maxi-dresses, and not in the mood to try to lose weight to fit into any of her pre-Sophie wardrobe. I felt the need to take a mental health afternoon and hang out at the mall with her. The carousel in the center of the food court mesmerized Sophie. Trina promised that if she behaved, we would come back and take a ride. After lunch, we headed toward the dress shops.

We stopped at the kids play zone between the food court and our shopping goals. Since I had the entire afternoon off, I wasn't in a hurry to go anywhere. I had no problems sitting with Trina while we watched Sophie climb, slide, and spin. It was actually good, because I wanted to talk about David and Peter. I couldn't believe I was having men problems between my boyfriend and a ghost.

In low tones, so all the other moms sitting around couldn't hear, I told Trina about when David and I did the deed, and how Peter stood there, watching us and yarding off.

She cackled. "Only you would get a pervy voyeur of a ghost, only you."

"Shut up, Trina." I leaned in and whispered, "It was so fucking hot."

She let out a fake gasp. "You did not get turned on by a ghost yanking his own chain."

"I was already on, and cranked to the max." I might have blushed. "And his chain is a beast."

Full on perv mode. So, you thought me watching you was hot? Hmm, 'cause it was sexy as fuck watching you get off.

I froze. Peter's deep voice sounded right in my ear as if he sat right next to me and leaned in just as I had done with Trina.

I'd like to see your face while I'm the one making you moan like that. If he hadn't have surprised me, I would have blushed more. I felt like I did the opposite, all color bleeding from my face down to my toes. My throat went dry.

"You okay?" Trina asked, looking at my face.

"Yeah, weird goosebumps. Did it just get really cold in here?" I wasn't cold, but I had to think of something fast. I wasn't prepared to tell her Peter was present.

"I didn't notice anything." She went back to encouraging Sophie on the short toddler sized slide. "Okay, munchkin, Mommy has to shop." She lifted Sophie and cooed at her as she swung her into her stroller.

We headed off toward our quarry. Trina had three shops where she thought we would be able to find a dress. Peter walked right behind me, off to the side. The sound of his voice in my head sounded like he was leaning in and whispering in my ear. I had all the sensations without the tickle.

Are you going to ignore what I said? His tone was low and teasing.

It seems safest. I though back.

You looked like you wanted me as much as I wanted you. Did you think about me while your man was on top?

Stop, okay, just stop. This was a hard conversation to have, I clearly needed to establish those boundaries I had been pissed off over. Peter was being sexy at me, as we walked through the middle of the mall. Granted, no one else could hear us, but it still felt out of place. I didn't want to admit to myself, let alone to him, that yes, I did think about him for a bit while I was with David.

I loved David—I had to remind myself that. That scared me. I shouldn't have to remind myself that I loved David. It should be a given.

The first store didn't really have anything that Trina felt flattered her figure. I had to agree. Peter kept making random comments about the clothes in the store. I got the impression he hadn't been dress shopping in a mall—ever. I could talk to him in my head, but I could not laugh without making noises. The sales clerks must have thought I was crazy. Hopefully, she thought I was laughing over making faces with Sophie while her mom tried on clothes. We achieved dress success at the second shop. With a reasonable dress acquired, we headed back to the carousel. Peter followed a few steps behind me.

Okay, I admit you're sexy. I confessed.

Peter made a satisfied chuckle sound as if he had won, and he had known he would.

But that doesn't mean you can do what you did last night. I love my David, okay. I'm not going to have fantasies about you while I'm with him. It's not going to happen. And I don't want you to manipulate my dreams either. I felt like I defended myself against any and all possibilities.

You can have your own erotic dreams about me, but I can't participate in them?

I don't have erotic dreams about you. I lied. *And if I did, they need to be my dreams and not you visiting my dreams and manipulating me. Look Peter, I can be your friend, and I will help you with this story rewrite of your life, but I can't. I can't pretend to have some kind of relationship with you. I love David, I'm loyal to David.*

I heard him sigh. *I admire your fidelity, and I respect your decision. As your friend, I'll back off.*

Thank you.

"So he's here, isn't he?" Trina caught me off guard with her insight.

"Yes, he is. Right behind me. How did you know?" I swallowed.

"There is a lot of paranormal activity in this mall. I was told there is a rift through a few stores over that way." She indicated with her hand the north wing of the mall. "Besides, Sophie keeps looking for him." She was right Sophie had been turning around and watching the space past me where Peter strolled.

Your friend is perceptive. His voice rumbled in my head.

"When did he get here, or has he been with you the entire time?" Her voice was even, never giving away that she learned a ghost followed us.

"When I got that shiver over by the play area. He just kind of showed up, making inappropriate comments."

Trina raised her eyebrow at me. "Well, you were talking about having sex with David."

I had no idea this mall had paranormal activity. I felt a

little skittish. That might explain why Peter was able to show up here. He said he could show up in places there was a strong tie to me. This explained why at work and why at home. But I had no connections to the mall.

We made our way to the restrooms before the promised ride on the carousel. I told Peter to wait and not to follow us. No one could see him, but I would know and that was something I did not want to deal with, no sexy straight men in the bathroom, please and thank you. Fortunately, he agreed and went to lean against the railing.

When we came out of the restroom, Sophie, out of the stroller, pulled us toward the beloved carousel. She went straight to the section of railing where Peter leaned. She stopped before she got to the railing and moved to an area about three feet away. There was no visible reason for her to do that other than to not stand in the same space as him.

I slid into the space immediately next to him. Trina scooted in next to me. "He's right there, isn't he?" she asked, looking into the empty space.

"Yeah, did you see what Sophie did? She headed straight toward him."

"I saw that. She stopped like someone's standing there, then moved away." Trina looked back at the horses at Sophie's command. "He's pretty benevolent, isn't he?"

"So far. I mean, I can see him if I don't look. And he keeps smiling at her."

She can see me.

"He said she can see him." I sighed and turned away from the spinning horses. This was all a little too strange for me—hanging out in the mall with my ghost. Actually, he was pretty nice to hang out with. He didn't complain about being in the mall and the people there. David didn't like malls, and was very vocal about going into one with me whenever I convinced him to come along.

"As long as he isn't freaking Sophie out, it's okay. She's not crying, so it's all good for now." Trina scooped Sophie up and headed for the rider line. "You coming?"

"Yep, I want to snag that dappled gray horse." I headed after her. Peter stayed put along the rail.

I enjoyed the ride, mostly because Sophie giggled the entire time and thoroughly enjoyed herself. I liked having Peter waiting and watching, and smiling at me every time my horse made its loop around. I'm not sure when Peter left, but he was gone by the time we got off the ride. We rode twice, before Sophie started her afternoon hyper-tired melt down. She wanted to keep riding. She needed a nap. She was done for the afternoon, and that cued the end of our trip to the mall.

6

I sat staring crossed-eyed at my computer. The morning's infusion of caffeine hadn't kicked in yet. I spent another night sitting in the middle of my bed writing into the wee hours. I really needed to stop this obsession. I was stiff from sitting on the bed and tired from staying up too late too many days in a row. I didn't write the entire time. I spent a lot of time reading back over everything. Did it make sense? What did I need to write to tie two scenes together?

I wasn't writing everything in the order it would be read, so I had to constantly check to make sure I included details early on that were considered common knowledge later in the story. I was probably going about it all wrong. I wasn't a trained writer. I didn't know how else to do this, and I wasn't about to audit a creative writing class on campus.

Some benefits of this job were that it allowed for up to nine free credit hours a semester. We were encouraged to take classes for personal and professional development. I probably should be pursuing a degree with my free classes, but I couldn't think of any degrees I wanted. I had the one I wanted and needed, plus all the extra credit hours for my specialty. Any art classes the college offered, I already had taken, that was the point of having gone to an art college— all art all the time.

"Gillian. Earth to Gillian." I blinked, I heard Holly in my head. Great why was Holly in my head? She wasn't dead. I panicked at the thought and spun around. Holly stood behind me.

"Whoa, space cadet," she jumped back, "what planet have been on? I've been trying to get your attention for at least five minutes."

I blinked at her. I had seriously spaced out—no wonder she laid it on thick with the space metaphors. "Ah, I was trying to focus on email. Wow, I really did zone out there. At least I didn't fall asleep."

Holly shook her head at me. "Here." She handed me a job folder.

I opened it and flipped through the contents. It was a job coming back for a second, or a third round of revisions after a client review. I knew that but I could not comprehend what the job was supposed to be about, or what changes needed to be done. I tossed the folder onto my desk.

"Is it too early to go get some coffee?" I asked. I really wasn't sure of the time, had I been at work for minutes or hours? I felt fuzzy brained. My late nights of reading and writing finally caught up with me and I was on the receiving end of a mental butt kicking.

"It's never too early to get coffee. Let me grab my wallet."

I was still in the same brain addled position when Holly came back to let me know she was ready to go.

I grabbed my wallet and we headed out.

We crossed the central quad and made our way to the popular coffee shop next to the student center. We could make a pot of coffee in the breakroom, but fresh air and a walk always helped to restore mental function.

I saw a student walk past with a large ice cream cone. I stared at it enviously. Now I wanted ice cream. Ice cream and coffee, that's what I really needed: sugar and caffeine. Fortunately the barista at the coffee shop accommodated me when I told her what I really needed. She made something that was more like a coffee milk shake than a mere cup of steaming caffeine, and she topped it with whipped cream in epic portions, and hot fudge sauce. It was exactly what was needed to jump start my brain. And to think, I had no idea they could even make a concoction of such delight.

Holly eyeballed my drink with open faced jealousy. "I should push you over and steal that," she joked as we made our way back to the office.

"We can always turn around and go order you one," I pointed out.

"No, I will stick with my small cup of half-caff, no cream, and half a teaspoon of natural sugar." She sighed mournfully while looking at my cup of a million calories. Holly was on the rounder side of body types. I know she struggled with her self-image at times. I'm pretty sure hanging out with no body fat me could be a real pain in the calories, especially when I did stuff like this, have a whipped confection of nothing but empty calories, and not have a single pang of dieter's remorse.

I would willingly trade her some of my caloric burning skills for some of her body fat. Especially if I could inject it directly into my boobs. Holly had a good boobs and a cute figure. She went in where women are supposed to go in, and she went out where they were supposed to go out. She wasn't a hard body. Unfortunately society has trained too many people to think that women who look a certain way are the only acceptable body types. Holly was on one end of the spectrum and I was on the other. Men could be real jerks about a woman's shape.

The caffeine, the walk, and the company did my head good. I was able to focus once I returned to my cube. The folder Holly had given me, before we took our break, did not fare as well. When I tossed it, it knocked over an old drink. The client notes were a blurred damp mess, the sketches completely ruined. I felt like crying. One stupid careless tired move and I made ten or more hours of work for myself. Ten hours I couldn't bill, and would have to explain to my boss. I didn't have time for this, I had a deadline. I decided to put it off and deal with it tomorrow. The rest of today was already allotted to a series of computer images that involved super imposing illustrated organs on top of photographs of different people. The illustrations had been completed the day before, today was all for the rest of the computer imaging.

I rubbed the back of my neck when I heard Peter.

You're burning your candle at both ends these days, Gil. That's why you're so tired.

Tell me something I don't know. I grumbled. *I know, but the ideas get into my head and they need to get out before I forget them, or they drive me nuts.*

I rubbed at my neck some more. *I wish you could touch me. I need a neck rub.* I whined in my head.

My eyes immediately started watering.

I guess that means you're actually trying to rub my neck? I asked.

It was worth a shot. You know I can feel you like a boundary. It's not touching exactly, I can't move through the same space you're in.

Interesting, but can't you walk through walls? Now I was curious, what were his limitations in this form?

I seem to, but I can't walk through a tree or a plant.

Living things. I noticed. *You can't pass through living things. But I can pass through you, can't I?* I tried to stick my arm through the space I thought he was occupying.

Hey! That's not easy on me. Normally it feels like a magnet repelling me, I get moved or pushed out of the way. But yeah, you can move into my space, I can't move into your space. It's a one way street, I guess.

What other cool ghostly things can you do? I chuckled.

I have incredible powers of observation.

That's 'cause you can get into my head.

It's called using my advantage. Peter smirked.

Fine, advantage boy, what are today's keen observations?

You are tired. Tonight you need to go to bed on time. No writing.

What are you? My mother? I asked like the smart-ass I was.

No, I'm a wise old man.

Old, yes, wise, not so much. I snorted.

Peter was right, I needed rest, and to not be up so late again.

I made it home after a very wimpy workout. I ate a simple dinner of rice, shrimp, and steamed veggies drowned in teriyaki sauce. It sounds fancy, but the shrimp were pre-cooked and frozen, the veggies I had already chopped on Sunday, and the rice was already made. I microwaved everything in stages, and then drowned it all in sauce.

I sat and ate as I mindlessly watched soccer with Mike. He couldn't tell me who was playing, but the goalie in red was delicious. I put my dishes in the sink then headed to bed. No writing. I tried to text David for a few minutes, but he wasn't very responsive, so I said goodnight.

I woke up sore. At first, I thought I over did it on the work out, then I realized it was the tireds catching up with me. Another few hours in bed would feel great, but I had places to go and people to see—otherwise known as having to go to work.

It was a no makeup kind of tired day. Of course, as soon as I made it in and people began asking me if I felt well, I realized I should have at least put on some mascara. I dug out the mini mascara and eyeliner I kept in my purse and snuck off to the bathroom to put on some eye makeup. Apparently, it didn't help. Now, I looked tired but with makeup on.

It was going to be a long day.

I began trying to figure out how to save the sketches I ruined the previous day, for what I hoped, would be a final round of approvals before I began the airbrushing. Everything felt sore and crampy. I tried to do a few stretches before I wandered off to see if there was a pot of coffee in the breakroom. The caffeine and the moving about did not help. I really did need a full-body massage.

My boss called me into his office. My organs-on-people printouts lay on his desk. The look on Adam's face did not say, 'These are terrific.' His words didn't either.

"Gil, look at these." He slid the images across his desk to me. "The client sent them back."

"Yeah, I did those yesterday. What's up?"

"You are a visual expert on human anatomy, are you not?"

I smirked, that sounded like a fantastic title. I should not have gotten cocky so fast.

"Please explain to me why that cis-gendered man has a uterus." He pointed at an image of a young, bearded man, with a full set of female reproductive organs superimposed over his lower abdomen.

I really looked at the images, finally seeing them. I closed my eyes and started crying. I didn't feel good—I was stupid tired, I hurt. I already screwed up one project yesterday, now this one.

Hours of intense computer work completely useless. Not only had I put the uterus on a man, I gave a little girl a prostate gland. Out of all of the images the only one I got right was the lungs on the runner.

Stupid. Stupid. Stupid.

"I'm sorry." I sniffed, not sure if I apologized for breaking down or for messing up.

"The client thinks you are completely incompetent, and has chewed me out for allowing this to happen." Adam sounded like he wanted to pass that chewing along, as it was, his stern voice was intimidating as hell.

I put my hand out to request the job folder. "I'll fix it. I'm sorry."

"Yes, you will. You're lucky it was delivered ahead of schedule."

I shuffled back to my cube. The project yesterday had taken four hours—today it took all of my time. I gave the corrected job files with printouts to Adam. I apologized for messing up again.

Adam flipped through the prints. "Job's done. Go home. But we need to talk in the morning."

I didn't walk so much as felt like a zombie dragging my dead limbs home. I was beat by my mistakes and worried about job security. My ego hurt. My head hurt. My whole body hurt. It was an incredibly long walk. By the time I got home, I didn't feel like eating. The thought of cooking anything was exhausting.

Mike insisted that I eat something. He put a bowl of lentils and rice in front of me and wouldn't leave until I ate some of it. After a few bites, Mike told me to go to bed. I didn't feel like arguing with him. I made my way to bed via my tub. I turned the on the taps and let the tub fill. A nice long soak in a tub full of hot water and lavender oil was exactly what I needed. I turned the water off and went to get my jammies.

As I slipped into bed, I realized I had a tub full of warm water getting cold. I think I was asleep before my head hit the pillow.

7

I burned hot like lava and froze colder than ice. I was hot. I was cold. I felt like crap. Well, no, not crap. Crap was soft and squishy and warm. I was none of that. I felt hollow in the back of my throat and everything had edges. My head swirled in figure eights, switching directions. There was no point in trying to focus. I had to keep still, except I could not stop shaking. I wanted to be warm and ignore the sulphur taste in the back of my mouth coming from my stomach.

I was too cold to move to find socks. Of course, moving to get socks would make my head start to twist and that would trigger my guts—best to lay still and hope to fall back asleep. I did not want my guts to get in on the action. No throwing up. Throwing up—bad.

It felt like hours of shivering, aware that I pretended to be asleep while holding still, I managed to finally pass out a few minutes before my first alarm went off. I couldn't move. Everything hurt. I knew if I waited long enough, the obnoxious beep-beep-beep-beep repeat would turn itself off. I managed to slip back into unconsciousness and ignore the radio alarm that began blaring.

"Gil, that racket has been going off for almost an hour, aren't you going to get up?"

I groaned, "Cold, don't feel good."

Mike came over and placed a cool hand on my forehead after he turned off my alarms. "Oh, babe, you're burning up." He walked away. I immediately missed him. Misery loves company. I realized that was not what that expression meant, but I was miserable and did not want to be alone.

He returned with a damp washcloth, some pills, and a glass of water. After helping me to sit up, he handed me a pill then the water.

"Where's your phone, Gil?"

I pointed to where it charged on my dresser.

"Who do I text?" Mike asked picking up my phone.

"Holly," I croaked.

I sank back under my blankets. I know Mike moved around a bit but nothing beyond that. I was taken by blessed sleep. At first, I had no dreams. Then I did, and they were weird even by my standards. When I woke up again, there was a pitcher of orange juice and a glass next to my bed, and Peter sitting by my feet gently petting my legs.

Gil, you need to get up and take something. I could hear him in my head as clear as every other time, as if he were actually in the room speaking. As usual, I could not see him if I looked. *Gilligan, you are burning up. Get up, Gil, come on, honey.* His voice was urgent. He really wanted me to move.

I clawed out from under my pile of warm blankets. I didn't want to move.

Gil, I can't help you, you have to do this. Peter coaxed.

I moaned. I did not like moving. Every muscle complained. Breathing hurt the top of my head. My hair hurt.

C'mon, honey, some medicine, then you can go right back to bed.

I wasn't going to move.

You probably need to pee anyway, he said on purpose. I have a very suggestible bladder, and clearly, he knew that. It worked. I didn't move fast, but I moved.

I swear my rug felt like it had been in the freezer, my toes were really cold. I shuffled slowly toward the bathroom.

Peter hovered behind me, following me in. I didn't care. I tinkled. That was it, barely anything, a few drops of liquid. I wiped, and then washed before opening the medicine cabinet. I grabbed a bottle of baby medicine before shuffling back to bed. Peter insisted that I sip some orange juice. I did.

It took some concentration for me to focus on opening the bottle. Once open, I sucked down an eyedropper of children's medicine, recapped the bottle, and lay back down.

I could tell Peter was inspecting the bottle. He would have picked it up to examine it if he could. Any movement he could enact on an inanimate object was always by accident, and never repeatable. It was nothing he could do on purpose, nothing he could control. I know it caused him a great deal of frustration.

Gilligan, this is for babies, it isn't going to be enough.

Clearly, he thought I was delusional in my current state. I was feverish and had focus issues, but I wasn't delusional. Most people asked why I kept baby medicine. I was appreciative that I could head talk to him at the moment. Making sound hurt my throat and head, but mentally talking didn't hurt so much. Of course, because I could talk to him at the moment didn't mean I was capable of forming intelligent, cohesive sentences. I like to think my conversation flowed smoothly, but I'm pretty sure most of my answers were really grunts and garbled word combinations.

Adult dose too strong.

Too strong? he asked incredulously. 'Too strong?' asked the man with an opioid addiction.

It's a redhead thing. It's either too strong or does nothing. I only need a baby dose for fevers.

A redhead thing, huh? Never heard of that before.

You're not a redhead. I groaned. *Too much talking.* I slipped back to sleep.

Every time I woke up, no matter how briefly, Peter sat there on the end of my bed watching me, petting my feet. He made sure I woke up long enough to take medicine again.

Sleep was always better than awake. In sleep, crows talked nonsense and I danced with polar bears in dump trucks. Awake, I felt like I had been hit by the dump truck. Awake or asleep, I was so cold. Until I wasn't.

At some point in the afternoon, I got hot. I kicked all my blankets off, and tried to peal my clothes off. It was as if my body went from Arctic conditions to equatorial vacation in the middle of a desert. Lava burned through my veins. I drained the rest of the orange juice, and made my way to the bathroom for cold water. I was hot and I was thirsty.

The heat was miserable and uncomfortable, and I had a hard time falling back asleep. Peter nagged at me to take medicine again. I did, my head was a throbbing bruise behind my eyes. Somehow, I managed to fall back asleep.

Someone tucked blankets around me the next time I woke up. I wondered how Peter managed that. "Peter?" I tried to ask. I'm sure it was just a croak of a sound.

"Don't let David hear you calling out some other man's name in this state, babe, I'm sure he will not understand."

It was Mike. He rested the back of his hand against the side of my face. "You're still burning up. I'm going to get you something else to drink. I see you got some meds. When was the last time you took that?" He fussed at me.

"When I was hot. Dunno," I slurred.

"Then let's hold off on taking more for a bit. I'll be back with some juice or something." Mike left me tucked in. I was still groggy and enclosed in my own personal fog bank of flu. Peter stayed with me, sitting guard, being vigilant.

I appreciated it more than I could express.

Mike returned with a pitcher of freshly made lemonade. It was cool and sweet, and felt good going down my dry throat. He also checked my text messages.

"Holly wrote feel better, and she told your boss you're sick. I'll let her know you are still on death's doorstep." I could imagine his thumbs dancing in a whirl of speed texting.

I managed to moan something in acknowledgment.

"David texted, nothing dirty. Doesn't the boy flirt with you? Let's see, there are about six messages, the last one asking if you're dead." Mike's commentary went quiet for a moment. "Okay, I told him you were sick and boyfriend needs to get over here and take care of you."

I could hear my phone text ping sound.

"Holly says she'll let everyone know, and if you, oh no, she means me, if I put a key under the mat, she'll come bring you some soup at lunch tomorrow. That's sweet. Okay, texting her to let her know that's appreciated. I like Holly, she's sassy. We need to have her over for drinks sometime."

My phone pinged again. Mike made a small gasp of incomprehension. He said nothing. Ping, again.

"Oh no, he didn't. Gil, you sure this boy is the love of your life, 'cause. Hmm-mmm-mmm." The last few hmmms, were clearly sounds of disapproval.

"What'd he say?" I mumbled.

"David said, and I quote 'text me when you feel better, I will see you then. Don't want to catch anything, take care.' That is not what someone's true love does."

I had to agree, that's not what I expected from him. I always nursed him and his colds by bringing him soup or a homemade meal when he felt ill. I even shoved a suppository up his ass once after dental surgery and the anesthesia made him nauseated. At the moment, I was really too sick to care. Mike took care of me, and Peter watched over me. David would have been in the way right then. Of course, my addled brain couldn't register that it should have been David and not Mike or Peter doing either of those things.

"You don't want anything to eat do you?" Mike asked.

The thought of food made my head spin and dragged my stomach along for a wild ride. I managed to groan negatively, my lips firmly welded shut. I was afraid if I moved or tried to make too much of a sound, things would try to escape.

"Ok, babe, you go back to sleep, I'll come check on you later." Mike fussed some more with my blankets before leaving and turning out the lights.

I drifted off in to a fever induced dreamscape. This time, I knew I dreamed about David, and Peter was there. Actually, he ended up being in a few of my dreams that night. I guess he was still keeping an eye out for me.

The next morning, Mike checked in on me. It felt like a smaller truck had hit me than the day before. Everything still hurt, but not as bad. I slept all morning with vague memories of Peter sitting by my feet.

Holly came over at lunch time as she said she would. She made me a bowl of ramen. It was that cheap college student staple, ramen, nothing fancy or ethnically diverse or old family recipe about it. Noodles and salty chicken broth, it tasted like ambrosia and helped me to feel better. Holly was chipper and filled me in on the office gossip, which really wasn't much, just who was stressing over what deadlines. Adam had given a few of my projects to a freelancer, so I didn't need to worry about anything except getting better.

"I still have a job?" I whined.

"Of course, why wouldn't you?" Holly asked.

"I fucked up those last two projects pretty good."

Holly fussed at me, made me drink some juice.

"That was a riot. I loved uterus man. I actually pinned that one up. Of course you still have a job, that client has a stick up her ass. So what, you goofed. You were way ahead of their deadline, and the fix was a no biggie."

"But what about the one I soaked in Coke?"

Holly smirked, "Oh, we gave those sketches to the freelancer. She'll be fine."

"But Adam said he wanted to talk to me, and then I didn't show up and. . . ." I felt like crying again. Why was everything so hard to deal with when sick?

"Pish, whatever it is, it isn't worth worrying about. You need to get better. And I need to get back to work."

After Holly left, I texted David. I wanted him to come over and sit with me after work.

"Not while you're still sick, I have big meetings this week. We'll get sushi when you're feeling better."

"Sushi? That's your other girlfriend." I texted back jokingly.

He knew I didn't like sushi. He had meetings, I guess that wasn't as bad as I thought with him not willing to see me while I was sick and needed care. I didn't want to be alone or burden Mike. I spend the rest of the day asleep. In my dreams, Peter lay down with me and held me. I liked the feel of him gently petting my head. I really didn't comprehend the significance of that for some time.

I had the flu for days. Eventually, I felt better enough to leave bed and drag my carcass downstairs to watch TV. Mike was a doll and made up a bed on the couch. I watched mindless TV, and slept through most of it. Peter no longer hovered around, and David still wouldn't come see me.

"What are you watching? Tarzan?" Mike asked as he handed me a mug of warm broth. He sat on the far end of the couch, eyes on the vintage man-candy black and white movie.

"Adventures of Sebastian Hale," I answered. The broth felt good. It would have felt better had David made it.

"Same difference." Mike was right, Sebastian Hale, Tarzan, He-Man, all the same, great white, shirtless, savior hero archetype.

I squinted at the TV. I needed to inject a heavy dose of this hero model into Johnny, without all the indirect racist and misogynistic crap.

By the fifth day of no David, I was pretty angry with him. I was sick, I was his girlfriend—so I thought, but I started to wonder—and he wasn't checking on me. That afternoon he surprised me and came over. Everything I was angry about disappeared as he took care of me. He arrived straight from the grocery store, bringing supplies like orange juice, applesauce, bread for toast, more ramen, and disinfecting wipes. He swept in and straightened up after me and my sick camp-out in front of the TV.

I mooned up at him as he used disinfecting wipes to clean off all the surfaces, and wiped down the remotes. "Thank you. I missed you."

He gave me a lopsided grin. "I missed you too. I had too

many meetings this week. I couldn't afford to catch anything. There might be a promotion in it for me."

"I understand." I thought I did.

"I'll be right back. Can you climb the stairs okay, or do you need help?"

"I can do it, but I go slow," I explained.

"I'll go get a tub started, and you head up when you're ready." He kissed the top of my head and disappeared upstairs.

It took me a while, and by the time I got upstairs, the tub was full of hot water, and David had pulled all the sheets from my bed.

"Hey babe, come on." He led me into the bathroom and helped me out of my sweaty jammies.

He gathered up my dirty clothes and left me to soak. By the time I was ready to get out of the tub, David had fresh pajamas for me, and my bed had clean linens.

Slipping into my clean bed, I wondered where he had been four days earlier. This was the responsible and attentive David I loved.

The last few days of the flu, I felt normal but weak. Returning to work, I had to field all the questions about if I had gotten my shot that year or not. I had. I also managed to get a different flu than the shot protected against. The upside of having the flu, my immune system was now supposed to be superior, and—knock on wood—I should expect to not get the flu again for a few years.

8

I looked at the list of work I had missed while I was out sick.

I had missed one deadline, but the department did not, thanks to my super anal organization skills at work. Adam was able to locate the computer illustration files and transfer them to the freelancer Holly told me about.

Never underestimate the necessity of an über organized computer filing system. Anyone snooping around on my computer can easily and immediately find all job files.

According to the list in front of me, I had about seventy hours' worth of work to get done in the next four days. My first step in tackling all the work was to divide it into two groups—traditional and computer. I prioritized them based on deadlines. Everything was wanted by end of day Friday. That meant I spent the next hour on the phone finding out if that really meant they needed it, in hand, by five PM Friday, or if they could wait until eight AM Monday. Fortunately for my sanity, but not my weekend, better than half were needed by Monday. I did have a few that were absolutely due Friday, they got slated to be completed first, then all the traditional mediums were scheduled, and lastly, the computer illustrations due Monday.

I wanted to get back to writing, since that didn't happen at all the week I was sick. It looked like that wasn't going to happen much this week either. My characters were becoming demanding in a way I could never have anticipated. They wanted out of my head.

I still wasn't feeling one hundred percent, so I was going to go for a slow but steady pace to make sure all my work got completed. The first set of illustrations was going to be used for an info-graphic by a designer. I needed to crank out a set of needles and injection sites, along with a set of stylized glands. I liked what I did for a living. I got to draw. I got to draw bodies and body parts, and I show people exactly what was going on inside us humans. I created diagrams showing how different organs, and body systems functioned. I created illustrations demonstrating how cells really worked. I had a really cool job, but sometimes it was just that—a job. Unfortunately, not everything I draw fascinates me, like needles, and flat stylized icons representing glands. This set of illustrations exhausted me.

As soon as I completed the first set of illustrations, I sent them out on the approval route. The needles and glands took more time than I cared to admit. I was tired and moving slow. The flu really had zapped my energy. I knew better than to expect to feel completely well right away, but I had not expected to be so wiped out. I hadn't had lunch yet, and I was fading. I shuffled out of my cubicle and knocked on my boss's door jam.

Adam faced away from the open door, tapping away on his computer. "Yeah?" he called out, not turning around.

"Hey, Adam," my voice sounded groggy even to me. He swiveled around, facing me. Adam loomed whenever he stood up. He looked like a tank more suited for football than art. Yet, he could create the most delicate and refined detailed illustrations I had ever seen. Somehow, he made the transition from science fiction illustrator to science illustrator to art director. His personality was as fine as his artistic skills—he was an excellent artistic director, time manager, and human. "I've routed the info-graphic pieces. I'm wiped. Um." I rubbed at my face. "Can I go home and take a nap, then come back and finish up?"

"Sure, Gil, you sure you'll be able to come back after your nap? You don't want to stay home?"

"No, I'm good, but I need a bit more than an hour to recharge. I'll be back in like two, two and a half hours. Like, I'm taking a really long lunch."

"Before you go, sit. We never did have that talk."

I swallowed, my stomach clenched. In my misery, I had successfully forgotten that Adam had wanted to talk to me about my colossal cock ups. I started to feel sick again.

"I've been thinking," he started. "We need to bring in a regular freelancer, take some of the pressure off you."

I sighed. Tension melted from my shoulders. "Yeah." I kept calm, mostly because I felt so wiped out. But inside, my little illustrator heart fist pumped and flailed its arms in an enthusiastic happy dance.

"The illustrator we had while you were out might be a good candidate."

"Can she start now?" I asked. "I'm gonna need some help catching up on everything and meeting some of these deadlines."

"I'll give her a call. You go rest. When you get back, pull all the files you want to pass on to her."

I started to tear up, I wasn't going to lose my job—I was going to get help with it. "Thanks Adam, I can do that."

"If you can't make it back after your nap, you call me." Adam sounded concerned, as he should be. If I was unable to work, deadlines still needed to be met.

"Absolutely," I confirmed. "When I get back, I'll go back over all the projects. I might need the help on one or two. I have three airbrushed pieces that need to be done in the next two days. I'd be happy to send over some of the computer pieces."

"Sounds good, come see me when you get back."

"Thanks, Adam." I shuffled back to my cube and picked up my jacket and purse. I slowly made my way out of the office. I stopped at Holly's desk on the way out.

"You are pale, Gillian, paler than normal," she told me.

"I'm going home to take a nap. I'll be back in a few hours. Could you call me to make sure I get up and come back?" I asked.

"Of course. Does Adam need you to come back? If you're still not up for this, we can make arrangements."

"No, no, I'll be fine. I'm just tired and moving slow. A nap, some soup, and then I'll be able to get in a few more hours of work. I need to pace myself."

"Sure thing, Gil, feel better."

I waved as I made my way out of the office. I found my car—not up to walking or biking yet—and made my way home. Fortunately, I lived close, less than a fifteen minute drive. I didn't even take my jacket off before I started my noodle soup. I became addicted to ramen during my illness. Ramen and apple sauce, the staples of my college and free-lance days. I felt much better after eating, but I still took a nap.

I slept hard for over an hour. My dreams were convoluted until Peter showed up. As soon as Peter walked into the dream, everything calmed down and made sense. He brought order to the chaos of my mind. The dream started off with dancing needles and flat two dimensional glands that looked like the animated playing cards from Alice in Wonderland. When Peter arrived, instead of everything swirling around me, it all became a stage show—strange musical theater, with music by Cole Porter and choreography by Bob Fossi. We sat in theater seats. He held my hand. It was warm and comfortable. His thumb traced soothing circles on the back of my knuckles.

I woke up with my phone ringing—Holly, calling to remind me to come back to work.

I made another bowl of noodles before I left, and grabbed a few cans of soda to take back with me. The drive back was quick, and I felt much better.

I stared at easily eighty hours' worth of work, and I had other projects still in the process. There was no way I was going to be able to take it all on.

I didn't like complaining to Adam, not without having thought a problem through. After my nap, I sat down and reviewed the impending work and the existing projects. I made an estimate sheet of hours I expected each of the new projects and the older projects to take. I had over three weeks of work on my schedule that needed to be completed in less than two full weeks. I'm good, and I work fast, but this was going to either require time travel capabilities, or extra hands. It's not like I didn't enjoy putting in extra hours at work. Okay, I didn't, I wanted to spend my free time writing and not drawing the detailed inner workings of the urinary tract.

I had two job folders in my hands when I approached Adam's office again.

"You look better, Gil, that nap helped," he said.

"It's what I needed." I handed him the two job folders.

Since I knew Adam didn't have access to a time machine that I was aware of, I prepared to beg for that freelancer, Jenny Spark. Fortunately, I didn't need to beg. "Do you think we could give these to the freelancer?"

Adam flipped open the folders, and quickly glanced at the contents of each. "Sure thing, you haven't started anything on them have you?"

"Not yet, do I need to provide sketches or can she handle it from start to finish?" I hadn't worked with this freelancer yet, I had no idea what her skill level was.

But Adam said she was available, but to do some sketches. I had time to collect the projects and do any preliminary sketches before handing anything over to her the next morning.

She was not what I expected. Most freelancers I've worked with have all had a bohemian style. Something about working on their own, or maybe it was that I was more comfortable with freelancers who fit the hippy description better. Even when I freelanced, I embraced the boho style.

Jenny Spark was not bohemian or hippy. She was more spit and polish and office appropriate than I was on the days I dressed "professionally." She had thick flowing golden hair, perfectly coiffed like a shampoo advertisement, and an enviable curvy figure. She wore a pin striped suit with a pencil skirt and a blazer. A little scarf was tied around her neck instead of a necklace, and the clear blue of her blouse set off her perfectly made up blue eyes.

I felt like a squished bug dressed for a day of being hunched over a computer drawing tablet. I wore stretchy yoga pants disguised as office wear and a knit top. Of course, as soon as she arrived I wished I had dressed up a bit more. I felt an immediate stab to my self-esteem. I didn't know what it was about her. She hadn't done or said anything to make me feel this way. My own insecurities were talking, making me feel substandard and awkward—stupid inner voices.

I smiled sharply and said, "Hi."

Actually, Jenny seemed really nice. She didn't take the job and go home, only to call me with questions. She asked if she could sit and review everything to make sure it was all clear. She looked around as I made space for her to sit down at my desk. She studied the pictures I had pinned up. One was of David and I, one of David alone, and then a picture of Peter from *Trouble Trouble*.

"Is this your boyfriend?" she asked pointing to the picture of me and David.

"Yeah, that's David." I half expected her to say he looked like the Doctor Who guy, most people do.

"He looks very successful."

"Um, yeah. He's doing pretty well, I guess." It was an odd compliment.

She continued to look at the images I had up. "Oh, he was cute wasn't he?" She pointed to the picture I had of Peter.

"He was." I felt a little embarrassed having his picture up like some fan-girl. I honestly had no excuse for it other than I liked to have something to look at when he talked in my head, made me feel like I could actually see him. "I'm using him as an inspiration model for a project I've been toying with." It wasn't a complete lie. I don't know why I felt the need to justify his picture being up. I didn't justify the pictures of the narwhales or the note cards with inspirational quotes.

I cleaned off a place for her, and she began reviewing the project while I got myself set up to begin the sketches I would digitize for the kidney and bladder illustrations. I dug out a few color chips for her when she was unclear on the specifications, and answered all of her questions—which weren't many. I felt confident that she could handle the bigger work load with the timeline we were handing her.

Jenny tucked everything into that slick black leather case of hers. "Thanks, Gillian. Can I text if I have any questions?"

"Yeah, sure." I jotted down my phone number on a sticky note.

She pasted it to the front of the job folder in her bag. "We should go have lunch when this is over. We can talk medical illustration."

I smiled. That actually sounded really good. There weren't too many of us who specialized, and the ones I did know where all much older. It would be good to make friends with someone my own age. Boob envy be damned. "I like that."

"We can go get sushi."

The thought of it made my stomach lurch. I'd have to talk her out of that one when the time came. I hoped my smile didn't falter too much.

"It's okay, Gil, she's pretty good," Adam consoled me.

He leaned on my cube opening, to check on me and what I thought of Jenny. He had no way of knowing I felt more defeated by her looks than her abilities. Unfortunately, in the past, I had lost out on jobs because of the other illustrators' personal appearance, or gender, and not because of their better illustration skills. I know because the people who hired the other person confessed to me, as they begged me to come in and save their butts on deadlines by doing emergency fixes on illustrations gone wrong.

I gave him a weak smile, spun in my chair, and got back to working on the bladder illustration. Hours later, when it was time most people started heading home, it was quiet in the office. I would be there for at least two more hours. I wanted to make sure everything was set up and ready for me to begin the airbrush projects in the morning. Fortunately, the sketches had been out for approval when I got sick. I needed to refine the outlines and start planning my masks.

Something about that woman was familiar.

I didn't jump. Peter's smooth voice eased over me, not freaking me out for once.

Familiar, huh? Maybe it's just you like curvy, well-dressed blonds? I teased. I was better at keeping the conversation in my head, and not accidentally talking out loud.

Not my type, but she is somebody's. I can't remember.

I shrugged. As long as she created decent illustrations, took some of the stress off my back, and wasn't gunning for my job—an actual fear that I realized was tickling me in the gut—I wasn't going to let her take up any of my brain. I needed all of it to focus.

You're feeling better. It wasn't a question, rather an observation.

Yeah, that nap really helped. Thanks for calming my dreams down. They wouldn't have been very restful otherwise.

What are you talking about? Peter sounded confused.

You didn't come in while I was asleep and make my dreams calm down?

No, I've been leaving you alone today. I figured first day back at work and all. You'd be snappy if I was in the way.

I don't get snappy. I thought about that for a minute, yeah I do. *I don't mean to get snappy.* I apologized.

It's okay, you try to stay focused, and I am a distraction. He announced his distraction status with grandeur and wide open arms.

Huh. I had to think about that, Peter had not visited me in my dream. Yet, he's who I picked to calm things down.

So, you're dreaming about me on your own? I could hear the smirk in his voice.

Shut up. I knew I blushed.

You're blushing. Why did he have to point that out? It only made the blush deepen. *Was it a dirty dream?*

"Shut up!" I snarled out loud. *No, it was not a dirty dream, just I . . . I thought it really was you, and I was grateful for your presence in the midst of the swirling weirdness.*

Well, I'm glad I could help even if it wasn't actually me.

I sighed. I was glad it was him too. I know he couldn't do anything, but I felt safe with his presence. It was nice to have him hang out as I worked. David never did that. Peter sat and twirled the chair slowly, poking at things on my desk. It was odd that he actually could get the chair to move, but never anything else.

The one time David visited me at work, he stood awkwardly in the corner. I huffed at myself. I was not going to play compare and contrast between Peter and David. That was ridiculous. David was real, flesh and blood, warm skin and toothy grins. Peter was, at best, a benevolent spirit, and most likely something made up in my head. But, since I clearly needed an imaginary friend, I kept him around.

I missed my boyfriend. Between being sick and having to catch up at work, I only saw him once in two and a half weeks. He wouldn't visit and hang out at work, something about that made him incredibly uncomfortable. Honestly, Peter acted more like a boyfriend than David did.

I was not going to let my brain go there. I was not going

to develop a crush on some ghost I made up in my head. Besides, if I had to have a crush on an imaginary character it would be Johnny Urban. He was more ideal anyway, no history with drug problems. I really created quite the guy with him—crazy good looking, crazy talented, and incredibly humble. Exactly what any girl would want. I still wanted to make him a were-tiger, for that added bit of bad-boy danger. Alas, Peter had very strong opinions regarding that.

I wanted to spend time with David, but it felt like the last few dates with him were nothing but booty calls. Part of me wasn't adverse to that—I felt the urge for another one. However, the part of me that was in love with him just wanted us to spend time together, regardless if we made love or not. I needed quantity time, not quality time.

There was a fabulous year round farmer's market near the condo, actually there were several in the area. David and I used to go and wander around them, sometimes, with no intensions of buying anything, simply an excuse to look at things and stroll. One of my favorites was this weekend.

"Hey, I got a small reprieve at work and I don't have to work the entire time. Wanna go to the farmer's market?" I texted.

"Really, Gil?"

"I could use an easy stroll in the fresh air. You know, rebuild my stamina."

He didn't text back for a while. I figured he was with a client.

"Okay, I'll meet you in the parking lot. What time?"

"You can't pick me up?" Parking was tight, he knew that.

"Shit to do afterwards. It will be easier if I can just jump in my car and go."

At ten AM, I sat on the trunk of my Toyota waiting for David "to come find me" like he said he would. I wore long walking shorts, a big brimmed hat, and huge sun glasses that gave me bug eyes. My typical outdoors wear included a rather unattractive UV fabric jacket. It wasn't my favorite thing to wear, but it was lighter than a regular jacket, and it saved the pasty white skin from the dangers of the sun.

"You really need to find a new stylist," David said as he approached me. A huge smile played across his lips as he teased.

"Hi stranger!" I waited for him to saddle up to me before I threw my arms around his neck for a kiss.

He gave me a quick peck, and then grabbed my hand, leading me toward the market. "How come I don't get you for the whole day?" I asked.

"James is having a beer pong tournament, and I agreed to referee," he explained. James was his younger brother. James was a classic case of 'you can take the boy out of college but you can't take the college out of the boy.' Only a few years younger than either of us, James still partied like he was in a frat house, majoring in beer buzzes. I could handle James in small doses. An afternoon of drinking beer was not a small dose.

"Ah, thanks for not including me." I really was relived to not be invited.

"So, how's work?" he asked.

I had paused to appreciate a flower display. Part of me longed for David to buy me some flowers. The part of me that bought my own flowers knew he wouldn't.

"I'm almost all caught up, finally," I said handing him my purchase. I bought a spray of mixed flowers. They were all tiny and in different colors. They looked like a handful of wild flowers. For all I knew, they were. "I still have to go in for a bit tomorrow. But Adam brought in this freelancer, and that's helping a lot."

I looped my arm through his, forcing him to slow down. I wanted to go slow, spend the time together, and I was afraid if I picked up speed I'd wipe myself out before we finished. I reached up and pulled a long hair out of David's collar. It had somehow gotten woven in with the fabric. I tossed it to the side, not thinking twice about it. David adjusted to my pace. We passed stall after stall of fresh organic vegetables. I wanted to kick myself for not having brought a shopping bag, but then again, I knew I wouldn't be doing a lot of cooking this week, so I didn't really need to buy vegetables only to let them rot.

I pulled a second hair from his shirt, and looked at it. It wasn't mine. It was the wrong color and the wrong length. I'd been wearing my hair in a short bob cut for the past year. The cut, with my figure, gave me a very nineteen-twenty's flapper style. I thought I looked cute.

A third hair—long and blond.

"Did your washer break?" I whispered.

"Why?" he whispered back.

"I keep finding long blond hairs in your clothes."

He chuckled, "Yeah, I had to go to the laundromat last week while the landlord fixed things."

"Okay." I knew there was a simple explanation.

The soap maker's stall was a feast for my nose. David started sneezing, so he stood back while I sniffed everything like a hound dog. I purchase two pounds of assorted blocks of handmade soap. I hoped they were as nice to my skin as they were to my nose.

"You aren't very chatty this morning." I noticed.

"I'm tired, work's keeping me busy," he explained.

"Is that why I haven't seen you? I mean this has been really hard, getting to see you."

He paused and turned to me. His hands cupped my face,

and he pulled my sunglasses off. He had the prettiest blue eyes, and they were looking at me. I sighed contentedly.

"It's only a bad patch, Gil, nothing to worry about." He kissed the bridge of my nose.

Our moment of bliss was interrupted by his ringing phone. After looking at the caller ID, he held up a finger to me and wandered off, taking the call.

I watched him walk off, perplexed. Since when did David tell me to hold on and move off to take a call? Normally, he held my hand and talked away as we walked. I decided to ignore it. I was being paranoid. I hadn't seen him in so long, now I started to feel like I was turning into the over sensitive, crazy, controlling girlfriend.

I found a curb to sit on while I waited for him to finish his conversation. Whatever it was, it must have been important. He was curled over into his phone, like he was trying to protect what was being said. It was a Saturday, so I doubted it was work, or something like a doctor's office. Maybe he was arguing with his brother. James could be a real ass at times. After a few minutes of watching David's back, I began people watching in general. I loved the variety in people, all colors and sizes and shapes. The farmer's market had a different mix than what I would normally see on campus.

I was lost in the swirling patterned of one woman's curls when David came back. He gently kicked the toe of my shoe to get my attention.

"Hi." I smiled as I looked up at him. He glowered, the furrow between his eyebrows deepening with his concern.

"I have to get going. I need to run some errands for James before I head over there." He held out a hand to pull me to my feet. "Sorry about this, Gil. I was afraid something like this would happen, good thing we have two cars, right?"

"Yeah," I sighed. We had barely been there an hour. "I

had hoped we could have lunch when we were done here. But, I guess not. Hey are we still on for next week at least?"

"What's next week?"

I wanted to kick him. This would be our third year of going to see Shakespeare in the Park. He should remember. I loved Shakespeare, and the group that did the park presentations was really top notch.

"Shakespeare in the Park, David, remember?" Clearly, he had not.

"Right, no, I hadn't. I can't next week. What am I missing?"

"Julius Caesar, you know—et tu Brute?" I sighed, frustrated.

"Next time, I promise. We'll go the next week." He kissed me on the cheek and left.

David was officially on my list. What list, I'm not sure. But seriously, he kissed me on the cheek? And he didn't even walk me back to my car.

I called Holly.

"I've been a crappy friend lately, you doing anything this afternoon?"

Fortunately, she was not. We agreed to meet at the mall. I wondered if Peter would show up and follow us around. He didn't. I liked Holly, even though we didn't do a whole lot outside of work, I didn't regret it when we did. I've had some work friends that were best kept at work. My stamina dictated that we stroll slowly. Holly was fine with that.

"Oh, you need to come smell this," she said dragging me into a tea shop. "You like the way things smell, you'll love this."

I had been telling her about the soaps I purchased.

One wall of the shop was lined in some of the most beautiful handmade tea pots I had ever seen. I instantly wanted to start a collection. They were so elegant. The other wall had large jars full of loose teas. A clerk hovered nearby waiting to assist anyone who wanted to dip into the contents.

Holly pointed at one jar. The clerk, a sweet faced young lady, unscrewed the lid, and using a small scoop, poured a small sample into Holly's palm. She crunched the tea up and put her hands to her nose. The expression of ecstasy on her face reminded me of a cat with catnip.

"Here smell." She held her hands out to me. She was right, it smelled wonderful and orangey.

Holly went through several teas this way. The clerk never lost patience with us as we oohed and ahhed over the smells. I ended up buying Holly an assortment of three of the teas. It was the least I could do since she had helped to take care of me when I was sick. Something my own boyfriend didn't even do.

"No, Holly, really, this is a thank you," I said as she tried to protest. "You did more for me than David did. And he's supposed to be in love with me."

We walked out of the store and began making our way to the Cinnabon, lured by our noses and their intoxicating cinnamon and sugary smell.

"Has he said anything to you?" she asked.

"No, he's busy with work, or hanging out with his brother." I thought about it. I had asked—those were his excuses.

"Maybe he's giving you space to feel better. You know," she clutched dramatically at her bosom, "he wants you so desperately it's easier to be away from you than to be near you and not ravage you constantly."

I snorted I laughed so hard. "Yeah, except he kissed me on the cheek this morning when he abandoned me in the middle of the farmer's market."

She stopped walking, the look on her face one of complete shock. "He kissed you on the cheek?" Her pointer finger dug into her own cheek. "The cheek?"

I nodded.

"Dump him." Her tone was matter of fact. "Seriously, what's wrong with him? The cheek?"

"Okay, so it's not just me that finds that odd."

"No, that's totally odd. He has hardly seen you in the past three weeks. He should be lip locking you every chance he gets."

I chuckled. I agreed with her. I wasn't mad at David, simply confused.

After getting our fingers sticky with cinnamon rolls, we continued to the end of the mall with the theater. We stood ogling the movie posters—hot men, fast cars, hot chicks, aliens, and space ships. There was quite the selection available.

"Wanna see something?" Holly asked.

I knew what she wanted to see, the car and gun show. And by gun show, I mean all the really buff guys with epic biceps.

"Absolutely!"

My afternoon with Holly had been a more pleasant date than my confusing morning with David.

9

Completely nude, with my hands resting on my thighs, I sat, kneeling on my bed. A large black crow stood in front of me. It croaked. This was a dream, and I knew I needed to be dressed. Instantly, I wore a white calf length dress. The cut was very nineteen-fifties, it had a boat neck collar, no sleeves and a full skirt. I had on a little pill box hat with enough netting to cover my forehead. Everything was white. I was in a wedding dress, still sitting back on my heels in the middle of my bed.

When I realized I wore a wedding dress, I looked up expecting to see my groom. The crow flew off my bed and morphed into a man. I was not surprised to see the bird turn into Peter standing there in a tuxedo. I smiled. The tux framed his square shoulders, and emphasized his lean build. His hair was a little on the long side, but it had been slicked back away from his square brow and his eyes, his beautiful big brown eyes. He was the right groom for me. In a typical standard weird dream transition, we were dancing in the middle of a large room, and I smiled up into his eyes. We held each other and swayed to some music. As we danced, crows flew circles over us. I smiled into Peter's eyes again, this time, he wasn't in the same body. Same Peter, only now he was taller and darker.

The dream transitioned into something else, and I lost the thread of what happened. By the time I woke up, I had forgotten everything except the part with Peter. I felt profoundly sad as I realized I had some heavy feelings for him. If he were imaginary, I could keep my feelings in check. If he was real, that was going to be a challenge. I wasn't exactly cheating with Peter, but if I accepted him as real, I needed to let David know what was going on.

Two and a half days passed before I finally received a text from David.

"I messed up this weekend, didn't I?" His message asked.

I hadn't heard from David since Saturday morning when he abandoned me at the farmer's market.

"Yes." I felt that I deserved a bit more than a text message apology.

He needs to take you out to dinner. Wine and dine you properly. Peter suggested.

I agreed.

"You owe me a proper dinner date." We needed to clear a few things up in our relationship, my expectations, my ghost.

"I do. Wednesday. I'll pick you up at from work?"

"Yes." I left it at that.

I didn't feel like chatting with David over text. He really should have picked up the phone and called me. He should have been on my door step the next morning with mimosas and waffles. Wednesday, that gave me time to make up my list of discussion questions and memorize them before I saw David again. Holly helped me to see that something was up with him. I already got the feeling Peter didn't like him much either.

Over an hour on the phone with Trina on Sunday, and she confirmed Holly's suspicions. I was being too nice to David, letting him get away with something. Even Peter agreed, and I hadn't asked him for advice. He nosed himself into the conversation.

Gilligan, you need to catch him out on what it is. I have my suspicions, but I'm not going to plant that seed in your head. You still love him right?

Yes, of course. I kicked myself, I shouldn't need to 'of course' regarding my love for David, but I was.

If you flat out ask him if he still loves you, he will say he does, so you can't do that. Peter offered.

Well, what am I supposed to do? Even in my head, I whined.

Get him to talk about work, anything. The more he talks, the more you'll find out. If you ask him a bunch of questions, it will be too much like an interview, he'll suspect something is up. Whatever you do, don't ask him if he wants to start seeing other people, unless you are prepared for him to do exactly that. Getting dating advice from a straight man was very different than dating advice from Mike. Mike was fast to kiss, faster to sex, and fastest to breaking up.

Waiting for date night to roll around turned me into a worrying stress monkey. A date with David shouldn't have been so nerve wracking. Even with plans on finding out what was really up with him and confessing about Peter. I spent hours trying to decide what to wear. I went through every dress in my closet at least twice. Without the time or budget to shop for something new, I finally settled on a slightly fancier than work wear dress with long flowy sleeves and a scandalously low V-neck. Of course, it was purple, my power color. We had been together for a few years, we should be comfortable together. So, why wasn't I? It was easier being around Peter in my head than with David. Maybe I felt guilty over Peter. There was nothing to feel guilty about. Or was there?

David picked me up as planned. I slid into the passenger seat of his car, a new-to-him used Lexus. And by new, I mean since the last time I had been in his car. Had it really been that long since we had seen each other? This vehicle was swank—leather interior, real wood paneling.

"Wow, David, this is really nice," I said appreciatively, petting the dash in front of me.

"Thanks, I thought it suited my status better."

"Did you get a promotion at work?" The step up would make him a regional supervisor. That meant less time traveling to do on site repairs for the ultra-sound equipment he worked on.

"Not yet, but this tells them I'm serious." He boasted.

"It tells them something." I wasn't sure what it would tell his boss, but it told me he was over extending his credit.

Over dinner, David told me all about the extra work he had been doing. All the additional groups he was working with to get noticed by the higher-ups. I commended him on his new found ambition, a character trait I can't say I had ever really noticed in him before.

He apologized several times for neglecting me the past few weeks, but big things were headed his way, and soon. He could tell.

He behaved more like we were on a first or second date, prim and fussy table manners, hair uncharacteristically slicked back, strained smiles. It wasn't until I told him about the ghosts that I saw my David.

"You what?" David roared with laughter. This was not going well at all. I had expected him to get all quiet and thoughtful, maybe even a little weirded out like Mike had over the cat. I had not expected him to snort wine through his nose and laugh at me.

I tried to ease him into to whole concept of it. I started off with how when I was in college, I started seeing Mr. Cat, the large black one. David nodded along and ate as I explained how the cat always seemed to be walking around corners, or I would find him curled up in patches of sunlight.

"I always thought there was something a little spooky at your condo. What does Mike think of the cat?"

David seemed skeptical, but slightly open to the whole concept. It wasn't as bleak as I had anticipated.

"Mike was a little freaked when he first started seeing the cat," I explained.

"He can see the cat?" David asked incredulously.

"Well, yeah. Mike can only see the one. There are actually two cats now. Um, I don't remember when the second one started showing up, but yeah. Two cats one black, one ginger and white."

David nodded at me, his eyes a little wider than normal.

"So you believe me?" I glanced at him out of the side of my eye. Then, I took a bite of my dinner.

"Why not, ghost cats. So yeah, I believe you." He shrugged.

I felt positive about this—time to up the paranormal on him a notch.

"I also have a Thing," I started.

"What kind of thing?" He mumbled around a mouth full of food.

"Well, it swims," I began. I had to use my hands to describe it, "at about this level off the floor" I indicated right around three feet high. "It's big and grey, and slow moving. I don't know what it is, probably a fish, or maybe a dolphin. And when it swims past, I can feel the water around it, and everything gets really cold." I looked at David. I didn't know what he would do. He had been open enough about the cats. I still worried.

He nodded, and then smirked. "You have a large ghost space manatee following you around?"

"Well," I felt chagrined. The Thing was large and rather creepy, calling it a space manatee made me feel like I lived in some rainbow colored, overly bright coloring book world full of unicorns and whales swimming in the sky. I huffed at him.

"I'm sorry," I could hear the laughter in his voice. "You're being serious. But that does sound rather," he crossed his eyes and twirled his fingers, "woo-woo, Gil."

"Woo-woo or not, I have a Thing. And it swims." My tone was sharp. "No, it doesn't follow me around, I'm not surrounded by a host of furry ghost creatures like some demented cartoon princess. I'm trying to let you know about some strange, and serious, but very real shit in my life." I wasn't playing, and I wanted David to stop playing.

"Okay, okay, I'm sorry." He tried to placate me by petting my arm. It worked. "Sounds like you have more than a Thing and some cats."

"I do." I bit my lip. "I have a dead actor who hangs out with me at work. And he's the reason I've been writing."

He failed at suppressing another snort. That had been really hard, and David laughed at me. He didn't even try to stop or act embarrassed about it. He laughed. Loudly. Fortunately, I hadn't jumped all the way in telling him about Peter. I hadn't given him a name, I definitely didn't tell him who Peter was, only that he was a dead guy who was helping me write the story I had been frantically working on the past few months.

I knew then I would never tell David that Peter was Peter Keith, dead celebrity, especially after that reception. I didn't tell David that Peter was helping me write to "fix" the mistakes he made in the past. I didn't tell him how Peter had been there when I was sick but David had not, and I certainly did not tell him that Peter had made sexy time interesting by watching.

I sat there glaring at him. I stopped eating, and stared. I was done with tonight, and I think I was done with David too.

"I'm sorry, babe, I'm sorry." He apologized repeatedly, and bought me dessert.

I hadn't forgiven him for laughing at me. But I no longer hated him, and I completely rescinded my thoughts about breaking up with him over this. Okay, so he didn't fully believe me. It was a little on the strange and unusual side of things, even for me.

Once he realized he had over stepped the line laughing at me, David became very attentive. He used a low and soothing voice, leaning into to my neck to talk, tickling me with his breath, whispering sweet nothings to make me blush, and kissing my ear.

I let him seduce me with his words and his touch all the way home. I needed *my* David. It was hard to take my mouth off of him as we made our way upstairs. His lips were warm, his hands were firm, and it had been a few weeks since the last time we had done this. We both needed some physical affirmation of our relationship.

We played with each other slowly, enjoying the tease and reveal as clothes were lovingly removed from each other's body. David lowered me to the bed, kissing me thoroughly as he did so. He slid into me smoothly, and I expanded around him, gripping him with internal muscles. He slowly pulled back then eased deeper. We kept a slow, hypnotic rhythm going, no need for speed or frantic pounding. When David lowered his mouth to my breast, I saw Peter in my head.

He had eyes of flames. He reached forward and grabbed David by the neck.

David screamed and pulled out, standing quickly, all while reaching for his neck.

"What the hell?" I yelled at Peter.

"God, my neck," David responded. He paused, then tilted his head to the left then the right, stretching his neck out.

"You okay?" I asked David, all while I continued to scream at Peter in my head.

What the hell do you think you're doing!

Peter glowered at me.

You don't get to decide when I have sex with David, he's my boyfriend. He's been around a lot longer than you, and he will be around after you've taken off. You know what, right now is a really good time for you to take off.

Peter stood there in the shadows. I could sense him breathing hard; he wanted to hurt David. His voice was ragged, snarling. *Protecting you. Ask David about the blonde, Gil, who is the blonde?*

David was already in the bathroom, I could hear him

start the shower. Our romantic mood killed by a pain in the neck named Peter.

What are you talking about? I sneered.

He's been seeing some blonde. I caught something in his memory. Ask him, it's the blonde I saw in your office. Peter clenched his jaw.

I closed my eyes. Peter had said Jenny looked familiar. I sighed deeply, I didn't want to know. Peter had never lied to me, even when I had been a whiney bitch to him, he had never lied. So why would he make this up? I slowly made my way into the bathroom.

I stood outside the shower. I watched David's silhouette as he showered. "How do you know Jenny, David?"

"Huh? Jenny? Sparks? The illustrator?"

"Fuck me," I spit. How the hell did he know her? Was he the one who told her I was out sick and they would need someone to pick up my slack? "Yeah, the blond medical illustrator, how do you know her David?"

David said nothing. The water shut off and the curtain opened. "About that," he said slowly. The expression on his face was all I needed to confirm everything.

"You're fucking her?" I grabbed my head with my hands. "She's why you got that stupid car you can't afford, isn't she? Oh God, and the hairs on your clothes, they aren't from a stupid laundromat." I looked around for something to throw. I picked up a bottle from my sink and hurled it at the shower. It smashed into the wall. Perfume filled the room from the scented lotion, as the white goo exploded on impact. I threw a towel at David, and instantly wished it had been harder so that it hurt when it smacked into him. "How long?"

"Gil," he pleaded.

"How long?" I growled.

"I met her at work, about a year ago. She was—"

"Get out," I hissed before walking back into my bedroom. I grabbed a bag from the back of my door, one I hadn't yet taken back downstairs for shopping. I ignored David who frantically dried off, and filled the bag with all the things he kept for when he stayed over. I returned to the bedroom, and emptied the side table drawer that was his. It mostly had condoms we no longer needed—I had an IUD now—extra boxers, and a fresh T-shirt.

He had most of his clothes back on when I threw the bag at him.

"Gil, I'm really sorry. We—"

"Get out."

He never once denied it. I sat on the edge of my bed staring at my feet. I wanted so desperately at that moment for Peter to come and fold me in his arms and continue protecting me from the idiot David. I curled in on myself and fell asleep.

In my dream, Peter paced around my room, guarding me.

The next few days were spent in a fog. I had a hard time focusing. I really loved David, or rather, I had. I had felt like we might have been drifting a little, but not enough to start looking at dating other people. I thought if anything, it was a rocky patch, nothing more.

I didn't cry over David, not once. David had been cheating on me, he didn't deserve my tears. When I did cry it was because I felt like I wasn't enough, I wasn't worth being loved. I cried over wasting my time. When I cried, I hurt so badly.

I cried for days. At work, when I wasn't sniffling, I had the hiccups. I cried when I told Holly what a bastard David was and how stupid I had been. I cried when I told Adam we couldn't hire Jenny anymore, not after what I found out about her and David. I cried more when Adam agreed with me, and said no one gets to mess with his illustrator and get away with it. I cried when I saw Trina for our weekly lunch. I cried when I realized I was making Sophie sad and she started crying.

I was a mess.

I didn't cry when I listened to David's lousy excuses he left on voice mail. I didn't cry when I texted him to put all my things in a box outside his door, and I would pick them up in the evening. Originally, I had thought about telling him to throw all my stuff out. Then I realized I had some sexy underwear at his place. Expensive, sexy underwear. I wanted that back.

A few days passed with me either crying or being mopey. It wasn't conducive to creative thinking. The illustrations I produced at work were serviceable but not my best. The writing didn't happen at all. My two guys at home were great and kept me company. Funny to think the two most stable men in my life at the moment, the ones I could count on, where romantically unavailable to me. Mike was gay, and Peter non-corporeal. Mike hung out and watched mindless TV with me, and when I sat in my room doing nothing, Peter hung out with me. It was like no one wanted me to be alone.

I didn't cry when Peter was around. I was morose, depressed, melancholy, but I did not cry. We talked about gloomy things. I finally asked Peter to tell me about how he died. I never had asked before.

Ya know, I know how I died, but I don't remember dying.

What do you remember? I asked.

My last living thought? Pain. I wasn't in pain. I had been but then I wasn't. I couldn't tell you if it had been a physical pain from my back or that all consuming pain of needing a fix. I needed something for the pain. The world hurt, he explained. I could understand that concept, the world hurting. Right now, my world hurt.

Peter was quiet for a while.

You don't need to tell me. I was just curious. I hadn't looked it up, and I realized I was thinking you had died in an accident.

Accidental overdose. I couldn't remember if I had taken a pill or not. If I had, it wasn't working, so I took more, he said, his tone flat. *Gil, are you going to be okay?*

Yeah, I will. I'm just sad. I don't miss him. I'm not even really angry at him.

You should be furious, Gil. He was using you.

I could tell from the tone of his voice, Peter was mad for me.

Using me, but not loving me. Why not? What's wrong with me? Why don't I get to be loved? Huh, Peter? I tried, and failed, to not cry.

I turned to look at him, forgetting momentarily that he wasn't physically there. Not being able to reach out to him when I needed the comfort was an extra stab of pain.

You are loved, Gil, right now everything is too raw for you to feel anything but the hurt. You are surrounded by love. Trust me on this one.

I huffed, a small chuckle. *I do trust you, Peter, I really do. I love you, Peter, you're a good friend.*

Go to sleep, Gil.

It's early, I complained.

You're tired, and this has worn you out, go to sleep.

Peter did something, he somehow pulled the dark over my eyes and I fell asleep. The sleep was much needed.

10

"Gil, are you sure you're over David?" Mike asked.

I spent the past week crying and being angry. I was done. Time to stop wasting any more time on that man. I handed him my heart and was too stupid to notice when he had given it back in a box. He had been a coward there and left it on the doorstep without even a note.

I was okay. I really was.

"Yeah, I really think I am. I have so much other love in my life, I don't need David."

"Convincing yourself?" he asked.

"Not at all, it's just that this has been coming for months, I was just too stupid to see it at the time." I tried to be honest with myself, and really, the past four or five months of dating David had really been nothing but a series of booty calls. Yes, I was convincing myself.

"But is dating a good idea?" Mike sat on my bed, having provided wardrobe consultation services. I finished up my hair and makeup in the bathroom.

"It's not a date-date. It's a double date so Holly can go

out with this guy. I'm being a dating accomplice," I explained.

"Does your date know this?"

"Does my date care? C'mon Mike, Holly is setting me up with the loser friend of some guy she met online. If he's good looking, I'd be shocked. If he doesn't live at home with his mother or talk about anything other than video games, I will also be shocked. Actually, I have a running scorecard with Holly. I'm basically expecting two to three week's free lunches out of her for this."

Mike chuckled. "Ah, dating bingo. Have you set up a betting pool for how soon into the date he asks if you'll have sex with him?"

You will not sleep with him, Gil. Peter's voice was a deep growl.

I jumped, my eyeliner suffered from the jerk reaction.

Geez, Peter, I didn't even know you were here.

I calmly grabbed a cotton swab to fix my makeup. I could almost catch his reflection out of the corner of my eye —but not quite. I got the sense he paced like a caged tiger. He was definitely angry.

"Loser buys margaritas next time we hit happy hour," I answered Mike out-loud and in my head I answered, Peter, *Calm down. No, I'm not going to sleep with anybody. I'm not like that.*

Good, he growled.

I didn't know what his problem was. This past week he had been so supportive, so sweet. Now, he was a snarling monster. *When did you get here, how much did you hear?*

Mike said you'll have sex with some guy.

Oh c'mon Peter, not fair getting all mad when you come into a conversation that's already happening. I am going on a date to do

Holly a favor. I expect it to be horrible, yet entertaining. Are you happy now?

He harrumphed. Cranky old man ghost.

"How do I look?" I spun for Mike as I came out of the bathroom. I thought I heard Peter mumble 'beautiful,' but he was already gone. I went with a glamorous-goth ensemble tonight, a black lace dress and too much black make up with bright red lips.

"You look fabulous." Mike hugged me and then headed downstairs. "Don't do anything I would do on a first date." He popped his head back in the door. "Seriously, Gil, you know what a slut I can be. Don't do that."

I laughed as I grabbed my handbag then headed out to go meet Holly and Mystery Date Man.

She stood looking cute in a bright orange dress with white piping, her dark hair curled down her back. We were color opposites, my orange was on top.

"Hey Gil, you're just in time. I think our table is ready," she said as I stepped up to the group.

"This is Rich, and his roommate John." I shook hands with each of them.

Based on posture, and how he positioned himself, I determined that Rich was Holly's date. That meant John was mine. I turned a smile to John. He had a sneer across his face, and a chin beard. Not my favorite look. I basically had no boobs, so I wasn't going to be too judgey on someone's outward appearance. He could be perfectly nice, and not realize that the sneer coupled with the chin beard was not a good look on him.

"How are you doing tonight?" I asked with fake enthusiasm.

He gave me a once over and did not hide the smirk he gave his friend.

The hostess called Holly's name, and we followed after her like ducks in a row. John brought up the rear.

"You shave?"

I turned around and gave him the best 'what the hell did you just say?' look I could muster. "Excuse me? I don't think I heard you correctly."

"You shave?" His eyes made a pointed stare at my crotch. "Down there? I mean, how am I supposed to know you're a real carrot top?"

I may have given him a chance despite his outward appearance, but all bets were off now. I know I blushed, and not because of his flirting—if that could be called flirting. I blushed because of the amount of volcanic steam that my head had to contain before exploding.

"Not like you're going to find out," I snarled through clenched teeth.

We took our seats and the hostess handed us menus.

"Get what you want, I'm not paying for you."

"Wouldn't dream of it." I kept my tone happy and lilting. Anyone eavesdropping would hear pleasantries in my tone, and not the murderous rage I felt.

"So Rich, you and John are roommates. You don't happen to work together too, do you?" I asked because I didn't want the torture of saying another word to John.

That was the opening of the flood gates, and the moment Holly plastered her grin and bear it smile on for the duration. They did not talk about the predicted video games, and I didn't win a bingo score for living in Mom's basement. But they did bitch about the servers at work and used really specific computer-related jargon, so I know they weren't talking about our waitress. They might as well have been speaking a different language. I don't even remember if either of them asked Holly or me about what we did.

We left as soon as was polite after dinner.

Holly and I agreed we both lost and would be buying each other's lunch next time we went out. At least the second half of the evening was a success. We took ourselves over to the nearest Mexican place with a bar and got nachos with our well-earned margaritas for having survived the date. By the time we were done for the evening, we laughed hysterically at the awkwardness of the whole date-fail. Neither of us would call it a date—that might imply that something good had come of it.

Standing in the middle of the kitchen, I gave Mike a quick recap of the terrible date when I got home. He howled with laughter.

"Poor guy really doesn't have a clue, does he?"

"None. Do you think he realizes that not everyone shaves all their body hair off? I mean, clearly, he didn't." I gestured at my chin indicating the unfortunate mange of a beard John had.

Mike shivered. "Better you than me, I might have dropped trou to show off the jungle garden I am cultivating." Mike did a dramatic pose, spun like a pop star in a music video, and opened the fridge to look for a snack.

"Goodnight, Mike." I slipped off my shoes before climbing the mountain of stairs.

"Night, Gil."

I dragged my butt upstairs to get ready for bed. I wiped off my makeup, brushed my teeth, and then took a shower. I fell asleep almost before I finished buttoning up the front of my pajamas once in bed. Peter waited for me on the dream plane. I recognized this was not a normal dream.

"I don't like it when you sleep with other guys." He sounded rough, like he had trouble controlling his emotions.

I scoffed, "I noticed." I sat up in bed, expecting him to sit by my feet as usual.

He stood there, staring at me. His arms crossed over his chest.

"I'm serious, Gil, I don't want anyone else touching you."

"Look, Peter," I said as I crawled out of bed to stand in front of him. I prepared to wag my finger at him, giving him what-for. He had no claims on me, and really, what was he going to do about it? He's a ghost.

I had forgotten this was his domain, he could touch here. He was corporeal here.

Peter wrapped his arms around me, pulling me to his chest, and then claimed my lips in the tenderest kiss. His lips were soft and warm as they caressed mine. At first, I didn't react. I was too shocked. Then I melted into him. A million butterflies swarmed in my tummy. The skin covering my body tingled. I couldn't believe he touched me, and I was more than thrilled to touch him back. My arms snaked around his neck and I began kissing him. I clung to Peter as if he were rescuing me, and he pulled me to him as if he could somehow merge our bodies into one.

His hands were warm as they clutched at my back, firmly grabbing me, like a massage. Yet, so gentle as he began stroking my hair.

"I can't handle it anymore, Gilligan." He held my head forcing me to look at him. His eyes were so full of pain. I would do anything to help him. "I can't handle knowing you're out there looking for someone else when I've been right here the whole time."

"Peter, I—"

His lips crushed mine again. When he pulled back, he searched my face.

"I was with David. I couldn't have, I wouldn't have. There were boundaries in place I would never have crossed."

"No more David, no more boundaries?" he asked.

"No David, no boundaries," I confirmed.

There was more want, more need in this kiss from both of us. I didn't realize how much I craved him until then. I thrust my tongue into his mouth, wanting to taste him more thoroughly, wanting to finally lick his teeth. He tasted like warm spices and citrus. His tongue danced with mine, and I welcomed him into my mouth.

His hands cupped my face before they began trailing down my arms, then on to my back. His arms tightened around me, crushing me against his firm chest. I began tugging at his shirt, pulling it from the waistband of his jeans so I could run my hands up the skin of his back. His skin was so smooth. I could feel the strength of the muscles underneath. Tonight he chooses to be physically perfect and young.

He broke away long enough to pull his shirt off. I inhaled sharply, appreciating the proximity and the view of his glorious chest. I tentatively placed my hands on his pecs. His muscles felt hard, solid under warm skin. He closed his eyes and sighed at the contact. Chest hairs tickled my fingertips as I ran my hands over him. Boldly, I ran my fingers down his flat firm abs and tugged the front of his waistband. Peter thrust his hips forward, and I began working the button free and undoing his zipper.

I snaked my hand into the front of his jeans. Commando! My fingers found him, he was so hard. There was nothing else between me and his flesh. I wrapped my hand around his growing erection and squeezed.

"Ah, don't break it," he moaned. I must have squeezed harder than I realized in my enthusiasm. I laughed, removing my hand before I shoved his jeans from his hips to his knees. Peter kicked them off the rest of the way.

He was glorious—tanned tawny skin and lean defined muscles. Crisp blond hairs covered his chest and a darker thatch surrounded his long, thick manhood. I was able to touch it all. I could feel and smell him. I breathed him in, he smelled of clean soap and a hint of Old Spice. I pulled him on to the bed and on top of me. His weight was sensuous, an erotic pressure. Perfect.

My hands ran all over his body, down his back, over his backside. I had never touched a body so toned, so firm before. Peter continued to kiss me, one hand cupping my head to him, the other slowly kneading a breast through my pajama top. His hand left my breast, but his lips were firm against mine. Slowly he found and began unfastening the buttons to my top. Once open, I could feel his chest against mine, this time, skin to skin. Peter broke the kiss and pulled back. He looked at me, my eyes, my lips swollen with his kisses, then down at my exposed breasts. Without a word, he pulled back more and yanked my pajama pants off. I squirmed out of my top, leaving me in panties. Those were pulled off next. I swallowed, my mouth dry as I watched him visually assess my body. I swear I could feel his eyes on my skin, like a firm caress. His eyes raked over me from head to toe, then back to my face.

I knew Peter had mostly dated curvy, buxom starlets with dark hair. It was a type he seemed to prefer. At least, that's the type he was always photographed with. Even if the hair color changed, the body type didn't. He seemed to prefer little waists and big boobs. This was the moment, which in my past could really defeat me as a human—that first time being completely nude with a new lover. I went for relationships over casual sex for a reason, emotional connections didn't care about physical attributes so much. I bit my thumbnail, waiting for the comment about my small breasts, my pasty white skin, my narrow hips, or my naturally red hair. It never came.

Peter let out a ragged sigh and clamped onto my lips again, ravishing my mouth with his tongue. His hands caressed and stroked as much of me as my hands were doing to him. This kiss was even sweeter to me, he hadn't said anything negative. He had paused to look, and from his hooded expression, he had appreciated what he saw.

As we continued to kiss, his hands found their focus— breasts, and butt. He caressed and teased my flesh. He pinched a hardened nipple, causing me to moan into his mouth. Slowly, he began kissing along my jaw and down my throat. He left little bites along my collarbone.

A loud moan escaped my lips when he sucked a pink nipple into his mouth, rolling his tongue around the taut peak. He moved his hand, caressing my hip, then his fingers were stroking my pubic hair. I was nothing but nerve endings. Anticipation caused a riot amongst the butterflies in my lower abdomen as I waited for his fingers to continue moving closer and closer to my core.

Two fingers slipped between my folds. My hips bucked. I tried not to call out. He continued to pet me, all while teasing my breasts with his mouth, tongue, and teeth.

I had one hand bunched in his hair, the other grabbing handfuls of blankets.

When he slipped those two fingers lower and then into me, I levitated off the bed. His thrusting fingers and sucking mouth were all I was aware of. I covered my mouth with a pillow so as not to scream too loudly.

When his mouth joined his fingers, I sang opera.

His fingers and his tongue worked magic. His tongue

laved my delicate flesh as his fingers thrust rhythmically, driving me to orgasmic heights. A peak that he held me at until I thought I would pass out from exhaustion. I had always thought orgasms were reached then done, like a timer, "Bing bing bing, it's over." Not with Peter. Apparently "bing bing bing" was just the beginning. I had no muscle control as he continued to suck and lick and thrust screams from me. By the time he was done, I felt like a limp noodle.

I swear he had to have been breathing through his ears. Or did he even need to breathe?

He kneeled above me, the most satisfied grin crossed his face. His fingers trailed back and forth between my hips. I shivered with each tickle. I was still all nerves, and they all screamed to be touched more. I felt replete. I felt drained. I felt the universe forming around me, stars colliding and creatures walking from the primordial ooze to dominate their worlds. I was so sensitized I could feel a ladybug breathe.

"I knew you were a screamer," he chuckled.

I panted, "I don't think I can move." I was spent.

"You don't need to, but a little encouraging action might help." He stroked my sex with his cock. I shivered in antici-pation. He pushed into my opening, easing in as I was more than ready for him. I moaned in satisfied delight. He was hard and thick and filled me in a way I had never been filled before.

"I'm not going to need much encouragement," he growled, grabbing my hips as I tried to meet his thrusts. Hooking his hands on my shoulders ended up providing the best leverage. I couldn't help but continued making noises as he rode me to his orgasm.

He didn't scream, but he growled out my name. That sent me over the edge again, and I came around him in explosions of electrical shocks. Peter collapsed on my chest. He looked like he couldn't move either. Peter rolled onto his back, dragging me with him so I lay across his chest.

"Gillian," his finger gently stroked my cheek. My name sounded like a caress.

I placed my hand on his chest, then rested my chin against it so I could look up at him. "Hmm?"

"No one else gets to touch you, okay?" His voice was thick with emotion—or was it exhaustion? Probably both.

"I might be able to agree to that, as long as you agree to continue to touching me like this," I teased. There was no way I was interested in finding anyone else. I certainly didn't think anyone else would be able to touch me with the skill he had. Why would I even want to go looking?

We made love a second, and a third time before Peter let my dreams morph into the oddities they typically were, and I got much-needed sleep.

I woke with a start. It was late morning, fortunately, it was the weekend so I hadn't missed anything, like work. Realization of my actions drowned me like a riptide. I gasped for air as I curled into myself, sobbing. What had I done? I finally had found my ideal match, my perfect lover, and yet it had to be the most colossal fuck-up of my life.

I realized why breaking up with David hadn't been so hard. I had completely and totally fallen in love with Peter. I didn't think I could ever tell him. How was I supposed to live a normal life now? Where were his comforting arms now, when I was awake and needed him most?

11

After the first few days of making love all night long, and I do mean all night, I found it hard to concentrate at work. Even though Peter could put me to sleep to enter the dream plane, it wasn't actually sleeping. My body thought it was wide awake. I was tempted to call in sick so I could stay home and sleep. I didn't. I was still feeling pangs of guilt for having missed an entire week with the flu, and that had been a while ago.

Hi, Lover. Peter's voice purred deeply in my ear. My eyes watered heavier than normal. I guess he leaned against my back or touched me somehow. I hated that I could barely sense him. I hated it more that I couldn't touch or feel him.

Hey, Pete. I wanted to be able to turn and kiss him on the cheek or smile into his eyes. I would had he been corporeal.

What's that? It looks like a diseased stomach. He wasn't wrong on the diseased part, but he was way off on the body part. It was a heart.

Your anatomy sucks. I laughed in my head. *It's part of a heart. Upper left ventricle.*

Gimme a break, his accent came out more as he relaxed

more around me. *Last time I had biology was the eighth grade. Be glad I knew it was a body part.*

You knew it was a body part because you know what my job is. I wouldn't be drawing it if it wasn't somehow related. I teased.

I only know what your job is because for some inexplicable reason I am drawn to being with you as much as possible. He teased back.

"Yeah." I sighed contentedly.

I was glad for whatever reason that had drawn him to me. I was glad for whatever it was that kept him around.

What are your lunch plans? He asked as if we could go out together.

I'm taking a nap.

Good. He purred.

Without you, I said pointedly. *I need to sleep. I haven't been getting much lately.* I blushed at the thought. I could hear him chuckle.

I finished outlining the section of the heart I was working on, printed out a quick note, and headed over to Holly's desk.

"Hey," I said as I approached her. "Can you call or come wake me up in forty-five minutes. I'm about to pass out."

"Sure, you look exhausted."

"Not sleeping well," I explained

"It's okay, Gil, you'll get over him soon. Life will return to normal and get better."

I let Holly think I was still reeling from the break up with David. That was fine. It was easier to excuse any excessive or abhorrent behavior I exhibited as missing David. Blame it on the breakup. It actually made more sense and was certainly less crazy sounding than what was really happening. I broke up with my no good cheating live boyfriend and began sleeping with a phantom lover. Yeah, that all sounded so sane. There was no way I would ever tell Holly what was really happening, at least not on purpose, and not while sober.

"Thanks," I smiled at her, "I know it will take some time. I mean we were together for three years."

"You holding up okay anyway?" she asked.

"I am. I'm gonna go pass out now."

I smiled and waved as I returned to my cube. I pinned the note I printed earlier on the outside of my entry. It said, "Shh napping, do not disturb." I penciled in the times I would be unavailable.

I put my head down on my folded arms. Darkness crept in behind my eyes. I felt the pull to unconsciousness by Peter, but he wasn't there once I fell asleep.

I woke with Holly jostling my shoulder. I slept hard and drooled on my arm.

"Better?" she asked.

"Um, yeah." I rubbed my face, and got up, yawning.

"Thanks," I said as I stood and stretched.

She let me sleep for about fifty minutes. Perfect timing.

"I'm gonna go wash my face and inhale a sandwich."

By the time I returned to my desk I felt refreshed, fed, and ready to finish that heart illustration. I put on my headphones, popped the tab on a Coke, and got to work.

You sing off key.

I hadn't realized I was singing along with my music. One of the more interesting aspects of being able to talk directly to Peter in my head was that I could keep my headphones in and still hear him clearly.

I'm an artist, not a singer.

Good nap?

Yes, thank you. Have I told you that's quite a talent you have, pulling me to sleep? I sighed.

Yes, several times in fact, but you don't normally sleep.

I bit my thumbnail and tried not to blush at the thought of all the not sleeping we had been doing lately.

I enjoy not sleeping with you, Gilligan. I'm finding out what they say about redheads is true.

Oh yeah? I asked.

Yeah, the carpets match the drapes.

I rolled my eyes. I heard that entirely too often in college but usually formed in a question as part of a drunken come-on.

And your fiery passion. He continued. *And eruptive empowerment.*

Are you telling me you have never been with a real redhead before?

Real as in real fake. Natural, apparently not. He chuckled.

I completely blushed now. I couldn't believe we were having this conversation while I sat calmly pretending to be working

I'm supposed to be working, you know.

But you're not, he purred, satisfied that he successfully distracted me.

I would much rather spend my time being distracted by Peter than working on cardiac illustrations.

I've got to work, deadlines. Will I see you tonight? It was a stupid question. Peter came to me every night since he claimed me as his. I needed to make sure he knew I wanted him to come back even though I was sending him away right now.

Get your work done, Gilligan.

My eyes watered as if he touched me, and he was gone. I missed him terribly the second he left. I wished I could kiss or hug him before went. It felt so dismissive this way without a gentle, loving send off.

~

The more I wrote, the easier it got. I seemed to instinctively know what had happened in Peter's life. I knew exactly how to change it up for Johnny's version of the story.

I spent a lot of time focusing on the interactions between Johnny and Michelle. Michelle was sweet, not manipulative. Peter helped me to develop the character to be as non-Hollywood as possible. She worked in an office, she rode the bus to save money and avoid the perils of parking. She had more squish than a hard-bodied starlet. She didn't have an agenda when it came to Johnny. She let him pursue her because she liked his good looks and personality. Through my pencil, their relationship grew.

What I had gathered from Peter, his wife had come with an agenda. She was a starlet and saw him as her gateway to an acting career. Michelle in Johnny's story was going to be loving and nurturing. According to Peter, his wife had been pushy and driven.

I sat upright. Hunching over notebooks in the middle of my bed was doing my back no good, but it was the only place I could write where Peter could show up and not be an issue. I read, then reread the passage again. I wanted to get the scene where Johnny met Michelle just right. Originally Johnny had been hitting on her with absolutely no reason for her to respond positively to him. He saw her on a literal street corner waiting for a bus, and he kept asking her if she wanted to go for a ride on his motorcycle.

Kind of creepy, actually. And then I figured it out.

I added in some Latino boys calling out rude things to her, and Johnny steps up and calls them out on their shit. Adding in the guys trying to hit on her, gave Johnny a chance to be Michelle's hero, and gave her a reason to agree for him to ride the bus with her. Johnny didn't have to do much, just enough to be protective to soften Michelle. After all, Johnny had been as annoying, okay maybe not as rude, but it was still unwanted persistent attention.

It wasn't a bad way to meet someone. I nodded in agreement with myself, I read the passage again. Maybe I needed to go in and rework some of it from Michelle's point of view. I knew she thought he was good looking, and she got a bit of a thrill when he asked her to ride his motorcycle. Something about a hint of danger with some good looking stranger asking to take her for a ride. But I hadn't conveyed that to the reader. The entire scene was from Johnny's point of view. Of course, Peter only ever shared his own point of view, so that made sense.

I don't know, maybe I should rework it. I could write the bus riding scene from Michelle's point of view. I know I wanted Michelle to fall for him pretty fast. And I didn't want to have a full year pass in the book before they finally got together. It was supposed to be a romance novel, they should fall in love instantly then spend the rest of the book bickering and fighting their emotions for each other, before finally succumbing to the realization they are deeply and truly in love.

Nope, not this time. This one is going to be a bit different. Their relationship will grow and develop, and it will be about that evolving emotional tie, even after they fall in love, and get married. It's going to be about a lasting relationship. So typical romance story plot lines were out the window. Screw it. I wasn't a trained writer, hadn't learned literary devices or rules. So it wasn't as if I purposefully breaking any of them. Hell, I didn't know if there were rules to follow to begin with. I did like that concept: rogue romance novel rule breaker.

Writing on my own without anyone to provide feedback was more difficult than I cared to admit. I wanted to show this to Peter. Other passages I had written with him around, so I could bounce ideas off of him as I worked. Trying to figure how to deal with Michelle on my own was tricky, doable, but tricky.

We didn't have a central plot that I could identify yet. Just Johnny and Michelle establishing a relationship, her family, and Johnny arguing with his agent over what roles would really build his career. Note to self: make sure he eventually fires that agent and accepts the career-defining role. Even Johnny's injury wasn't a major plot building make-it or break-it moment in the story. I thought about having Michelle get pregnant and the stress of Johnny's injury triggering a miscarriage. But it wasn't traumatic enough.

Every time I started to write a scene around this tragedy it never worked out. Johnny turned out to be accepting and understanding. I couldn't make him so angry he would want to leave her. I had the same situation with her. I tried to get Johnny hooked on pain killers, but instead of angering Michelle to the point of leaving him, she bucked up and helped him through the rough patches of weaning off the medicine. Michelle Cole was forming into a really terrific character, no wonder Johnny Urban wanted her. She loved and supported him without any extra drama. I could see why Peter wanted a woman like her. His actual wife had been nothing but drama.

I felt the pull to sleep in the back of my eyes before I even realized Peter was around.

"Oh, no, you don't." I tried to fight as my eyes rolled up into my head and I slumped back against the mattress.

"I had stuff to show you," I complained the second I saw his smiling face.

"You have stuff I want to see." He was such a tease.

"No," I spun away from him, dancing off the bed to get out of his reach. "I've written more, and you need to see it. You need to tell me if it works for you."

Peter lounged back, his arms folded behind his head. "Why don't you tell me about it?"

I crawled back up on the bed and sat cross-legged next to him. He was distractingly gorgeous, and mine. I could happily sit and stare at him for hours. He was better than some story. If he wanted this revised reality of his created, we had to do some work.

I lifted my hands with a shrug. "No notebooks, I can't read it to you."

He ran a finger over my knee. "Tell me, like a story."

I looked up at what would have been a ceiling in my bedroom but was a swirl of nebula clouds and stars in this realm. "Once upon a time," I started with a very put upon sigh.

"Lover..." Peter's tone had that admonishing hint to it. He wasn't mad, but I probably should behave.

"Okay," I lifted my hands in a 'here it is' gesture, and began.

"Johnny meets Michelle over a series of days. Always in the same place. Um, the first day it's raining, and he's just left his manager's office. Or maybe it needs to be his agent, anyway, he's on his Harley."

Peter shook his head. "He needs to be on an Indian or a Triumph. Something a little less mainstream."

I nodded. What did I know about motorcycles? Now, I just hoped I could remember to change it the next time I had a pen in my hand and my notebooks in front of me.

"He's on his motorcycle and it's raining. He's bitching to himself about idiot drivers in the rain when he sees her. She is the most perfect, most beautiful woman he has ever seen. Her face is a perfect oval with full lips and eyes like large black diamonds in skin the color of dulce de leche. And she is a freaking drowned rat because of the rain. So he pulls out of traffic and offers her a ride, which she declines."

"Smart woman."

"Exactly. This impresses Johnny. He has an umbrella from the manager's assistant and he gives it to the woman. He then says something dorky, and rides off."

"Dorky? He should be suave. I would have said something charming and made her laugh."

"Yeah, but you aren't Johnny Urban." I tilted my head and smirked at him.

"Are you so sure about that?"

"He says something dorky. Now, shush. The next day, he's leaving the same office and sees the woman again. He decides to check up on her, make sure she didn't catch a cold. She still refuses to accept a ride from him. This time when he leaves her he says the same thing again and realizes it's dorky, and he's become a cliché with a catchphrase."

"What does he say?"

"Something like 'stay safe' or 'safe journey.' Something like that. Now, realizing this is her bus stop, he sort of stalks her for a few days. Introduces himself, all that. He does this for the rest of the week, and even over the weekend. He's actually kind of clueless as to why she's not there over the weekend. She's been at that bus stop every day at five o'clock, so why not again on Saturday? He doesn't check on Sunday, having had an a-ha moment, but he's back on Monday."

"What happens differently, or did you write this up like a

montage for a film that needs to cover a lot of repetitive action?"

I thought about what he was asking me for a moment. "I think I just wrote it straight. I mean there is dialog and stuff so it's not as repetitive as it sounds. I mean like the next time he goes to see her, he actually takes a car to the intersection and is waiting for her to ask if he can ride her bus with her since she won't ride his bike with him. Wow, he sounds really stalker creepy."

"He sounds like he is pursuing a woman he likes."

"Yeah, but she's said no. He really should drop it and leave her alone. I mean if I were her, I'd start walking the extra mile or two to another bus stop. But this day is different, this time she sees him first. And she says hi to him. She does like him, he is ridiculously cute, and he seems concerned about her. And then this carload of Latino boys start catcalling her. They are tossing around all kind of Spanish epithets, and then Johnny steps up to tell the guys off, even though he doesn't speak a lick of Spanish. You don't speak Spanish right?"

"No, I don't," he chuckled.

"So now Johnny is Michelle's hero."

"But he didn't do anything."

"No, but he tried, and that's the point. He showed Michelle that she mattered. Especially since as soon as they drive off, he clues in that he's been a total asshole by hitting on her for all this time."

"What? A guy needs to be persistent," Peter said.

"No. A guy needs to listen to women and respect their boundaries. Johnny earns bonus points by realizing his own faults. Men owning their shit is crazy attractive."

"I thought women wanted heroes and big muscles." He lifted his arm and flexed his not inconsiderate bicep.

I sighed. "Big muscles are nice, but nothing is as hot as a strong man being vulnerable, apologizing, and not just being an asshole."

"So that's what Johnny does next? He says sorry and leaves?"

"Exactly, but Michelle stops him."

Peter's accent slipped and I heard hints of those long ah sounds so common in a New England accent. "I like where you're going with Michelle. She's very likable."

"She is." I agreed, surprised that I actually created a likable character.

"She's the kind of woman I should have fallen in love with," he stated, a hint of regret in his voice.

"What do you mean?" Happy that I created a sympathetic character, I needed to know how she was different, what was it about Michelle Cole that worked?

"She's supportive, yet reserved. She hasn't thrown herself onto Johnny expecting him to rescue her from the life she has. She doesn't have expectations of him because he is a famous actor. She's actually interested in having a family, and not giving him lip service."

"Is that what happened to you?" I asked.

"I fell in love with the wrong type of person. She wasn't in love with me as much as she was in love with what she thought I could do for her. My wife's idea of support was to provide me with drugs so I could keep working. Your character is nothing like that. I like what you're doing with her."

I beamed. High praise indeed. I bounced on the bed, jostling him. "Do I get a cookie?"

"Something better." He reached for me. "Come here."

I slipped into his arms, and suddenly waves crashed on the beach off to my right. I could feel a slight breeze. Peter hadn't brought me here in dreams for a while. It was that boardwalk he had liked. It had taken a while, but I finally figured it out—we were in Santa Barbara. He brought me here once or twice before he started really talking to me, back when he was still just a reoccurring dream.

Now that I was aware of his dream manipulation I paid more attention to my surroundings. I could see the waves, but I could barely hear them. I could see seagulls, but no noises came from them. I knew without even trying to deviate from the path, that I wouldn't be able to run onto the beach and dip my toes in the cool water.

If it weren't for the breeze, and the general ambiance for being outside, I would say we were on a movie set. It looked like we were actually here, but it was all an illusion. Illusion or not, it was nice to be outside and not have to worry about sunscreen, or getting a sunburn—there are definite benefits to this dreamscape.

Peter casually strolled. His hands thrust deep into his pockets and he smiled at me, easily laughing. I was not casually strolling, I bounced and walked backward in front of him so I could see his face. I flailed my arms around animatedly.

I was excited. I was making something out of words. Things were actually coming together.

"Why are we here?" I spun, the little sundress I wore twirled out, and I'm pretty sure I flashed Peter my panties.

"You are amazing. You are creating an entire world with words and your imagination. I wanted to bring you somewhere special. Do something a little different. Show you how impressed I am." He left the paved walkway and started out across a manicured lawn toward the ocean.

I skipped after him. I really could get used to this being outside without any of the consequences. I couldn't think of the last time I had been to the beach without sunscreen on, let alone with my shoulders and back exposed.

He continued to walk until we reached a beach picnic set up. A large blanket was spread out, and a colorful umbrella guarded over it, and two champagne flutes. Peter held out his hand to me and helped me to sit. He lowered himself into a lounging posture next to me. We clinked glasses and sipped the bubbles.

"Can I swim?" I asked.

He shrugged. "Why not?"

"I don't have a bathing suit." I indicated my dress, expecting him to dream-time me into a different outfit.

"You don't need one. This is a private beach, there is no one else out here. Just you and me."

"You mean skinny dip?" I was enjoying the whole not needing sunscreen, but, getting into the ocean naked?

Peter was up and pulling his clothes off. "Come on!" he called as he ran into the waves. He stopped when he was about knee deep and waited for me with his hands on his hips. He looked kind of silly. Hot, sexy, naked, and silly.

"Oh, hell," I muttered. I pulled the dress off and kicked out of the panties and skipped into the water after him.

Of course, the water was perfect. I splashed Peter and then dove in farther. He followed me and captured me in his arms. His lips were warm and salty wet. My skin slid against his, and suddenly his nudity didn't seem so silly to me. I wrapped my legs around his waist and he carried me back toward the shore.

Where the waves lapped the sand, Peter lowered me to the earth and followed me down to cover my body. Waves washed up and over our legs as we kissed and touched and twined together. Peter slid into me and I felt him and the ocean surge against me at the same time. As our tempo increased, the tide increased, as if the ocean responded to our thrusts and needs.

Wrapped in warm water, and Peter's body, I cried my orgasm into his mouth. As was his fashion, that was his clue to step everything up a notch. He slid out of me and flipped me over, tugging my hips up and back. I balanced forward on my hands, my butt spread toward the sea. A wave crashed into me and licked my sensitive flesh, all swollen and sensitized from his driving into me. I moaned. The ocean hit every nerve ending I had and felt like the lick of a wet tongue.

Peter laughed in triumph. And then he was pulling my hips to him, and thrusting. The waves and his balls caressed my clit in a syncopated rhythm that accented what his cock did to my core. As if the ocean had hands, I felt caressed over all over my skin. Peter reached forward and held my breasts, tweaking my nipples between his dexterous fingers.

I lifted up onto my knees and leaned back against his chest as he continued to drive into me, using the ocean like some kind of third member to our tryst. I came again, this time screaming out into the open. Seagulls returned my cries.

I turned in his arms, my mouth finding his again. "I want you in my mouth," I said as I reached down between us and stroked his hard length. He was marble covered in the softest velvet, and I wanted to taste him.

He lowered to his elbows back against the sand, and I watched as this time the water licked up his leg and tickled his balls. He hissed in appreciation, and I knew he had somehow turned the water into our own private dream sex toy. I spread my knees, so I could enjoy the ocean's licks as I lowered my mouth to his length. He was salt and seawater and the warmth that was Peter.

I found it hard to focus solely on providing expert fellatio because every wave caressed my folds and hit my clit seconds before running around the base of Peter's shaft. It only took a few times for that to happen before I was changing my position and kneeling over Peter's shoulders. If I was going to be licked as I sucked him down, I wanted his mouth on me. For added fun, he added his fingers without any prompting.

He came with a roar that tickled my flesh, and I pulled back, letting him come into the water. After he exhausted his orgasm, he grabbed my thighs, flipped me over and started all over again. Dreamscape sex was the best. He had the stamina and return rate of a porn star. I could go all night with orgasm after orgasm. We could scream and no one would hear us. And we could make love outside, on the beach, with no sand in sensitive places.

12

_____

"You are remarkably calm for having broken up with David recently," Trina said. We were having milk-shakes and onion rings for lunch at the Soda Shoppe, per our usual. I hadn't seen Trina for almost two weeks. Her husband had whisked her away for a surprise trip to Aruba, leaving Sophie with his mother.

I chomped on an onion ring. I toyed with telling her what Peter and I had been doing lately, but I realized that might not be the best idea. My sanity was in a delicate balance as it was. Trina needed vent time. She currently worked on undoing the damage that leaving Sophie with her mother-in-law had caused. I was a horrible listener, too wrapped up in my own shit. I "uh hummed" and nodded but my brain was on Peter.

I was fully convinced that I had a phantom lover, and just maybe he was really real. I didn't want to go back to thinking he was imaginary, because if he was, then my love life really truly sucked, and I preferred to be with something I made up than go out and find a living partner.

"It's been a few weeks. I gave David one week of my time

where I cried and I was mad and I texted him random cuss words. After that, he wasn't worth my time anymore."

"Seriously? You aren't hiding crying jags from me are you?" She raised her eyebrows at me.

I nodded. "Seriously. I'm really good. David was drifting away as it was. He was more involved with that other bitch." I covered my mouth realizing I had cussed in front of Sophie. A quick glimpse at her let me know she hadn't heard, completely distracted with her food. "David seemed to think he could juggle us both. He couldn't make up his mind which of us he wanted. I helped him with his choice, by removing myself from the equation." I ate another onion ring. "I've completely distracted myself with this writing thing with Peter. So it's good. Oh, you'll be proud of me." I started rapidly patting the back of her hand. "I went on a double date with Holly, it was dreadful."

I cracked her up with the tale of how bad that date had been. I did not tell her how my evening ended in Peter's arms. I sighed.

"You're the one who just went to Aruba, you should be doing all the talking. I need to shut up now. Tell me all about the island."

I listened intently as she waxed poetic about her week at an island resort. It had been one of those all-inclusive places, all she needed was a bathing suit and tanning oil. I thought dreamily how beyond nice it had been to go to the beach with Peter in his realm. No need worry about sunburn, and no one around so we could screw on the ocean's edge for hours with no sand creeping into butts and other places. I couldn't do real beaches very well being the sunburn victim that I am, but I love warm ocean water, and Peter delivered.

~

I was busy with my food prep chores, and Peter hung out on the bar stools yammering on about nothing in particular.

If he wasn't a ghost, it would have been a nice domestic scene. Of course, if he weren't a ghost I would have had him chopping vegetables too.

When we started talking about the book and Johnny Urban's life it felt like we kept crashing into the same wall, and now we're stuck on how to achieve a happily ever after. We were trapped in family planning land.

I don't understand why Michelle can't be pregnant again. Peter grumbled.

Because she just had a baby like three months earlier, and yes, I get that some people pop them out one after another. She's not going to have a big preggo belly and be breastfeeding a tiny infant at the same time. Biology was my thing, sometimes I forgot other people were just not as well versed in it. *If you want her to have a big pregnant belly, the baby has to be older.*

I see her as being so beautiful when she's got a baby in her. He sounded almost wistful.

I know you do. I think he really missed not having a wife who wanted to get pregnant with his child. From the tone in his voice that was something he really would have loved.

I continued to chop and we continued to discuss the merits of not having Michelle become pregnant a second time right away.

Where are we going with this story? I wondered, twisting the crank on the can opener. *We still don't have an acute conflict, and I'm not sure how it's supposed to end. I mean most romance novels end when they either get married or agree to get married. We've got these two happily married and making babies.*

Johnny hasn't returned to work yet. He's made the career movie, now he needs to make the epic come back film.

He should win an Oscar. Peter added.

Really? Action movies don't usually win those kinds of awards. I would think that blockbuster, opening week record-breaking earnings would be what we would want for Johnny. I dumped a second can of garbanzos into the blender.

I'll think about it. Peter said. I think he really wanted an Oscar, to have been considered a great actor. But the lure of top rated box-office hit was definitely intriguing.

You know if you let me make Johnny a were-tiger this whole acute plot-driving conflict wouldn't be an issue. A tiger would be the perfect beast for Peter with his blond hair and tanned skin.

Drop it, Gil. I'm not going to be some stupid shapeshifter.

"But..." I whined out loud.

Can't you just let this be my story? Keep it simple. No vampires, werewolves, were-tigers, fairies, wizards, or demons. Just the struggles of life, work, and building a relationship within those parameters.

I glared into the space where his shade sat in my brain. Fine, give up the shape-shifting and focus on Michelle loving him.

I checked the recipe I followed on my phone. I measured in some lemon juice, then two scoops of minced garlic, and a scoop of tahini.

That's new. Peter pointed his chin at what I made.

Yeah, I thought I'd make some hummus. Last week you missed my attempt at homemade salsa. It did not suck. I hit high on the blender. It whirled to life with a loud buzz-saw noise.

The combined goo looked too lumpy, not like the texture in the picture. I checked the instructions again and realized I had forgotten olive oil. After drizzling in the oil, I blended it again. This time the contents chopped and swirled together into a smooth paste. I stopped myself from offering some to Peter, which would have been rude. I do try to be politically correct around my corporeal challenged acquaintances.

I scooped a sample with a carrot. I smiled. It did not suck. I was getting pretty good at this adult cooking thing. Next week, I might even make both salsa and hummus.

By the time I finished cooking and prepping things for the week, we had made headway. I stopped pestering him about Johnny being a shifter, and we decided Johnny would continue with recovery and getting back into shape. Michelle would find out she's pregnant again when kiddo number one was not quite one year old. Johnny would stay home another year but would start doing voice-over work for video games. His new agent continued to search for the best return to the big screen movie for Johnny.

We hadn't really decided what kind of movie—a big action adventure, an Oscar-worthy drama, or something completely unexpected, like a musical. I sort of liked the idea of a musical, after all, Johnny Urban had been a teen pop sensation, why not bring that back?

I sat in front of my computer. I wasn't quite ready to begin transcribing all of the handwritten notebooks, but I had begun typing directly into a word processing program. I knew, in the long run, it would save me time. I also hoped that as my typing skills improved it would make the job of transcribing, what was now five spiral notebooks, all pages, front and back of handwritten story, a whole lot easier.

My fingers pounded away at the keyboard. My eyes

flicked between monitor and keyboard. I typed faster, but I still could not touch type. I'd love to say my fingers flew as I wrote about the happy day Michelle tells Johnny he has to recover; they are going to have a baby. But my typing skills were stilted and choppy at best. It was still a happy moment to write about. Johnny had slipped into a depression, hiding his pain, physical and mental, in bottles of pills. That part had hurt to write. I know it was Peter's actual experience he described to me. It made me want to travel back in time and smack him and smack his wife. Instead, I got to smack Johnny Urban, the fictional construct of my imaginary ghost friend.

As much as I believed Peter, as much as I had evidence to suggest that he was real. There was still a part of me that wasn't fully certain he wasn't just in my head. Imaginary or not, I thought this story he helped me to create was pretty good. Maybe Peter was really my muse? He was one hell of a sexy muse.

That thought stalled my fingers. I had never looked anything up about the life and times of Peter Keith. The internet was just a few clicks away. I could look. I saved the document I had been working on and opened a web browser.

I really struggled with putting his name into the search window. I started by searching for Johnny Urban. I mean it would be a shame if there really was an actor with that name. I'd have to change my character, and I didn't want to. I liked his name. The search came back with nothing. I typed in Michelle Cole. Whoa! That's a popular name. There were so many Michelle Cole's of every ethnicity—I did an image search as well—that I wasn't going to worry about her.

After building my confidence with those two, I typed in

Peter's name. The image search came first; his smiling face and big brown eyes repeated in different poses, picture after picture. Most of the images were from *Trouble Trouble*. He really had been popular. There were pages and pages of images. There were pictures of him older mixed in. I could still see his good bone structure under skin ravaged by sun and drugs. His eyes were the most telling, they had lost that gleam he had before the injury that started his decline. I switched to a search for websites. There were thousands of search returns. I started with the first entry, a basic bio from a popular movie database search engine. I continued to click and read. I found an online group that had been set up in honor of his life. I created an account and joined the group.

I must have read posts for hours. Post after post about how much they had loved Peter. Posts with only pictures of him, posts of fan art, posts of videos. I clicked and started watching: interviews from when he was young, fan montages, outtakes. He had been a handsome goofball. I read and watched everything on that page, it took hours.

I needed to show him this. I needed him to see that his fans certainly didn't think he had given them anything less than he could have. They loved and adored him. Somehow, he couldn't see that at all.

I tried to return to writing. I may have made Michelle a little over sappy, but I needed to give Peter the love he so dearly missed. Michelle's outpouring of love for Johnny was the best way I knew how to fix things for Peter. There are no do-overs in life, Peter could not go back and change his past. Hopefully, this fictitious fantasy of love and success would work the way he wanted it to. I didn't want it to backlash on him and make him sadder. I felt that somehow the success of this story, the completion of this story was connected to what he needed to be able to move on.

13

As the anniversary of Peter's death approached I noticed he became pretty cranky. I would like to think I understand why. I mean, it's not exactly an anniversary one would look forward to. I tried to show Peter the online group that was a commemoration of his life. He brushed it off in his short-tempered mood.

The story stagnated, making no forward progress. I felt obstructed by his lack of action. I couldn't very well move the plot along because Peter was the driving force behind the story. Anytime I took off with the plot and made headway it was always in the wrong direction. I didn't dare turn Johnny into a were-tiger no matter how much better I thought it would be.

Peter would show up and be pleasant enough. I could sense toothy grins and a teasing air about him, but something would happen and his mood would darken. I don't know what happened, I didn't know what I could do.

I started watching more videos of Peter, trying to get some insight into his personality. Trying to get some confirmation of a few things so I could continue to move forward with the story while he was being a crankmeister.

The online group was the best source for these videos. I have no idea how these fans found recordings of behind the scenes interviews from *Trouble Trouble*, or from the sets of the various movies he made. There were quite a few. And I watched them all.

I found one video where Peter was showing off an ankle brace disguised to look like a shoe and the scrape on his arm. I couldn't stop leaking. He sat there, wincing slightly every time he shifted—I could tell his back hurt but he wouldn't admit it—describing how he hurt himself. My jaw had to have been in my lap. It was exactly what he told me. Exactly.

I didn't know if I needed to be freaking out or not. I was completely capable of accepting that I had this ghost hanging around talking to me all the time, making love to me in my dreams, so why should I freak out now because I had confirmation? I have cats. I have a Thing. I have a dead celebrity ghost. Breathe, focus, it's okay, I can handle this. I went searching for more. Maybe if I had more evidence I'd relax about it.

There I was trolling YouTube for old afternoon shock jock talk show episodes. And I felt a bit guilty over it. Peter told me things regarding his life. And here I was fact-checking him. Why couldn't I accept what he told me? Why did I need to really find out the name of his wife? I mean I knew, he told me. At least I thought he had, I assumed Michelle was actually his wife's name and not just the name for Johnny Urban's love interest. But still, I needed proof.

I needed to prove that the ghost in my head was real and that I wasn't living in some sort of delusion. Part of me really believed that Peter Keith actually visited me and told me about his life. Part of me was convinced I was losing it.

I followed up on a group post that mentioned Peter had been on one of those "where are they now" child actor episodes. Doing a search on those videos made me want to stab my eye out with a fork. In true "oh-look-squirrel!" fashion I got distracted and sucked into many of the clips of the show. Most were along the lines of 'cheating boyfriend is really a woman,' and 'the secret sex life of BDSM little people.'

I finally found the episode with Peter. There were a few other aged kid celebrities on the panel as well. It was clear these were all has-been actors who could never quite get past the glory of their youth. Peter was no exception, even though he was, at the time they filmed that episode, a working actor. Of course, maybe, he didn't see himself as one. Going from A-list teen heartthrob to burned out, D-list if you're lucky, straight to DVD, made for television, and aired on obscure cable stations movies was probably not his idea of acting.

I know he had told me that he was embarrassed by a lot of the films he made, they were crap. If he could go back and re-do it, he would have fought for better roles, tried to stay in the soaps and not switch to B-movies.

Watching that talk show episode was tough. Peter was still good looking, but starting to slip.

He looked puffy and wasn't moving well. It was clearly shot after he hurt his back, and he had started his path to drugs.

The four panelists sat poised in their chairs: Peter, some chick from that all girls-school show, an actor whose show I didn't watch, and someone from even earlier in the late seventies. The older actor had made the transition from child-actor to producer.

I remembered him as a kid from some black and white show, never realized he was a redhead like me.

"You can't expect to be an actor forever. Look at me, I know I was hired because I have a baby face. I started to lose my hair in my late twenties. I was still playing teenagers on TV, with male pattern baldness." He chuckled then ran his hand over his mostly bald head. "You can still make it in the industry you have to reinvent yourself, change your role, change your contribution."

Peter countered. "Acting is better than any drug I may or may not have ever done. It's a hard habit to kick."

"Exactly," another panelist said in support of Peter's statement. "Look at that girl from Family Game. She did anything to continue acting. She's a porn star now."

The discussion continued, Peter was smart, he articulated his ideas and thoughts well. Why hadn't I stayed in crush with him? I could see why I thought he was intriguing when I was five. Why not when he was older? I know the truth. I was shallow. I was young—not to say I'm not still on the shallow side—this had been filmed when I would have been 15 maybe 16, and he was no longer pretty. He looked rough.

The first clip ended with no mention of his wife.

I clicked on Part Two. The first part of the discussion was skipped, I have no idea what they were talking about when Peter said "my wife Michelle." I couldn't hear anything after that. Their mouths kept moving, there was sound, but I registered nothing. My eyes streamed and my nose turned into Niagara Falls. I have no idea why but the truth of that simple sentence had me leaking like a rusty boat. I didn't cry, I leaked.

"Son of a bitch." I wiped at my face and tried to refocus on my laptop. I looked around to 'see' if Peter was nearby to... to what? Talk to him again? He had told me the truth, and it scared the crap out of me. I had to tell someone. I kind of wanted to tell him, 'Hey look there is this ghost of you, and you keep telling me all this stuff, little things. So, I decided to start checking you out online to see how crazy I was, and yet, I've found out that you aren't in my head. Well, you are but you're not something I made up.' What good would that do? He'd probably laugh at me.

Large black crows strutted around the quad, cockier than seniors. I hadn't seen this flock around here before, they really were strutting their stuff. Tall, pretty, iridescent and black, I always wondered if big crows like these weren't really ravens.

I walked across campus to the ice cream place. It was a nice warm day, and I needed some time alone. I needed to think, needed to get clear headed.

I had fallen in love with Peter completely, yet part of me knew I shouldn't. Part of me was terrified. Terrified to realize I was lying to my best friend about what was going on with me. Terrified to think what if Peter really was using me? After all, we had yet to work on my idea. Every time I tried to bring it up, he either dismissed me completely or most recently, he would try to distract me by dragging me to sleep so we could fool around. I was terrified to think that maybe my feelings for him were rebound emotions, after all, I had been so emotionally invested in David. And, I was terrified of what would happen to me if Peter ever got whatever it was to help his spirit move on to where it needed to go. It would be like he died, twice. I would be crushed, destroyed. This couldn't be the afterlife, no, there was something else out there. Hanging out with the living as a ghost was not the end-game to life. It couldn't be.

I sat on a low concrete bench. One of the cocky black birds croaked at me.

"Is that what you think?" I asked it.

It croaked at me again.

"I know, I know. I need to come clean with Trina. But, hey I didn't lie outright, I just didn't fully disclose."

Croak.

"Lying by omission, I get it." We stared at each other. Crows are wicked smart, I could see this one plotting against me. That, or it tried to analyze me. Most likely, it was eyeballing my ice cream cone. "How am I supposed to tell her? Oh, by the way, Trina I've been sleeping with the ghost of Peter Keith, and I found out he's not just something I've been making up in my head. It's not going to be that easy."

Croak, croak.

"Yeah, yeah, yeah, just do it. Suck it up cupcake. I hear ya. I didn't lie about David though. I really don't feel the need to spend any more time thinking about him and how he screwed me." But there I was, complaining about David to a bird.

Croak. The bird didn't move, it tilted its head at me as if saying 'I'm listening, keep talking.'

"I'm worried about that too. I mean, Peter doesn't seem to be interested in working on this book thing anymore. It's all sex, sex, sex with him." I smiled. It was good sex, sex, sex, but we did very little of anything else.

Croak.

I sighed. I was going crazy, I had an imaginary phantom

lover and I talked to birds. At least the bird was tangible. I could see it while I was awake and my eyes were open.

Croak.

"Really? Do you think I need to start working on the book on my own and not worry about getting Peter's input? Yeah, I've thought that too." I had, but I kept running into creative roadblocks. Peter was my muse, and it was easier to create in his presence. But in his presence, I'd rather do the other things.

I thought about Michelle Cole, my love interest character for Johnny Urban, and Michelle Cruz-Keith, Peter's wife. They were too similar. I thought about changing the names but then realized, there are so many women with the name Michelle in that age group it was okay. I had also thought about changing her looks and heritage. But I couldn't. Michelle Cole had to be Mexican-American, it was already an integral part of her character and the story. One of the minor conflicts of her dating Johnny Urban was religion. She was a Mexican Catholic. Her family pitched a fit until they learned he was raised Catholic.

I didn't realize right away that was straight out of Peter's life. His wife's family really had not been welcoming to the tall blond Anglo man Michelle Cruz had brought home. It wasn't until he mentioned something about not being available on a Saturday evening because that's when he attended Mass, that they accepted him. I was such a dolt, not realizing Peter was Catholic for the longest time. The Irish-American boy from Boston, duh. It also explained why they hadn't gotten a divorce, even though by all accounts they did not get along, and were having affairs left and right the last few years of Peter's life.

No, Michelle Cole was fine, she could stay as she was. Maybe I could start slipping in were-tiger aspects. I know

Peter hated that, but it brought in an extra level of excitement and danger. I shook my head. Staring at the crow in front of me.

Croak? It seemed to ask this time.

"Just thinking buddy. Realizing a few things, like I'm being a big idiot."

Croak.

I tossed the remainder of my ice cream cone to the bird. It hopped over, poked at it, and then began eating the cone. It looked at me again tilting its head to the side.

"You're easy to talk to, bird. Can I tell you a story?"

Croak.

I took that as assent. I began to tell the bird the story thus far with Johnny Urban. I needed to talk it out with someone, Peter hadn't been focused enough lately. I decided I really wanted to do this, write a book, even if it was just to see if I could actually do it. As I talked to the bird I found gaps in the story that needed to be filled. I also found a terrific way to open the book.

Currently, the action started before Johnny meets Michelle, but the story needed something to get the reader interested. Johnny was supposed to be a teen pop sensation. It was mentioned several times, it was an integral part of his character. He could sing, casting agents knew this, it was something that made him valuable in certain roles. But I had never written anything exploring that aspect of his life. Peter liked focusing on the aspects that were direct reflections from his life.

Acting, dealing with agents, and of course, making love to Michelle. I needed to explore more about Johnny being a pop star. Why had he made the transition into acting full time? There were plenty of popular singers that smoothly transitioned between acting and singing. Why completely ditch the one for the other?

Talking to the bird really helped my brain start cranking out the ideas as to why Johnny stopped being a singer. This was going to make a fantastic opening chapter or two. I knew it would start with a bang, a concert. The adrenalin rush, the sparkle cannons, the push of the audience sending all their adoring energy to the musicians on stage. The throbbing beat and pounding music. Yeah, this was going to be good.

"Hey, Gil, who you talking to?" Holly sat next to me.

"That big crow."

I pointed to the bird, but it was gone. Actually, all the crows were gone. I looked up in the sky to see if they had flown off. My ice cream cone lay where I had tossed it. Unpecked.

"Where'd he go?" I asked. "There was a whole flock of them."

"I don't see any crows, just the pigeon-rats, maybe you're seeing things. Hey did you know a flock of crows is called a murder?"

I got up enough to pick up the cone I apparently had tossed on the ground for no reason since there was no crow to feed, and sat back down. Great, I thought, I now had more spirit animals. I wish they could have been more helpful. I didn't feel like I had accomplished anything. Well, not true, I needed to come clean with Trina about my relationship with Peter, and I had worked out a good portion of the opening of the book.

"It's lovely out here," Holly stretched.

I agreed. "It is a nice day."

"I was headed over to the ice cream place, I know you already had one, but you want to walk over with me?"

I was tempted to say no, but I realized if I was left alone with my own head I was apt to start seeing more ghosts and spirits. I snorted.

"You okay?"

"Yeah sorry, thought of something funny. I think I'll have more ice cream." I snorted because I was becoming some demented princess with a host of ghost animals that I talked to—cats, a Thing, a Peter, and now crows.

14

I focused on a drawing when I felt Peter arrive. I tried to continue to focus on the inner workings of the kidney. This had to be accurate and not a stylized rendering.

He sat on the extra chair in my cube. I could see him plain as day in my head. He was in a teasing mood, he appeared as if in his late twenties. Hair slightly feathered in a mullet, not quite transitioned into the shaggier style. His jeans were stone washed and pleated, and he wore a pink Izod T-shirt with the collar popped up. He always showed up in what he thought of as the height of his good looks when he wanted to tease me. I really wasn't in the mood for it. It was my turn to be cranky.

The voice in my head was a clear as if he really were ten feet behind me. His tenor voice was smooth and confident. He wanted something.

Hey, Gilligan, Are you going to ignore me today? he asked

"Right now I am." I tapped the tablet to change brush settings in my program. I answered out loud. It sounded odd. I could completely hear his voice, yet when I spoke out loud the actual sound was harsh and distorted, like a speaker starting to go bad.

He played with the pencils in the tray of the drawing table. One of them fell. I jumped. I expected the sound in my head, it was loud and in my ears. I turned to glare at him.

There was no one there. The chair swiveled slowly as if it had been abandoned. A pencil lay on the floor. I picked it up and my blood froze. All the hairs on my body stood on end with an electrical discharge, and my eyes started streaming again.

I stopped and pressed my palms into my eyes. With my eyes shut, I could see him. He was completely there. He leaned forward

You ok?

Yeah. I had to switch to answering him in my head. Our one-sided conversations confused my ears. Also, I didn't need my co-workers to think I was any weirder than they already did. You know, crazy Gillian having one-sided conversations. *The reality of you does that to me.*

The reality of me? He looked at me like I was crazy. The look said, of course, talking to ghosts in your head is perfectly normal, why wouldn't I be real, why do you doubt me?

"You're real, you're fucking real." I bit out between clenched teeth as I sat back down and stared at the cubicle wall. I could no longer focus on the illustration on my computer, and I couldn't look directly at him. I wouldn't be able to see him if I did that. This way I could *see* him clearly.

Of course, I'm real. What you think I'm made up? he explained.

Oh my God, you bastard, you weren't lying to me! I wasn't leaking now, I was crying, trying hard to not freak out, and losing.

No, why would I lie? What do I have to lose by lying to you?
He was confused. I was confused. He was real.

Your wife's name really was Michelle, and she's Latina. I looked it up. That's a low thing to do to me you know.

What the hell did I do?

You made me think I was the one that made all that up off the top of my head. You encouraged me to think Michelle was a good name for a wife. You didn't exactly tell me straight up that you were real. I sniffed and wiped at my eyes. I was so mad at Peter. He hadn't lied to me at all. He really sat there in my cubicle and no matter what I did I could not look at him. I could not see him. But there he was. His hands were fanned out in front of him. Like he tried to steady me. I tried to throw the pencil at him, nothing. It sailed right past him. He didn't ruffle in a cloud of smoke, he didn't magically appear. But he was there. I could barely see him in my head, I just could not see him with my eyes.

I was mad. I was mad at him for being dead; mad at myself for allowing him in and talking to me; mad for falling for him. I was mad because this seriously freaked me out.

Hey! he barked as the pencil sailed past his head. *I didn't lie to you and you're mad at me? You make no sense.*

Why me? I wanted to look at him so badly, I wanted to see into those big brown eyes. I wanted him to touch me and pet my hair and say it was okay. But he couldn't, at least not right now when I needed it.

You showed up and started talking to me? Why?

You saw me, you listened. He sat there as I paced back and forth. I 'saw' him better if I didn't try to look at him. *Hey, I'm sorry about the whole Michelle thing. But yes, Michelle is my wife's name. That was the relationship I wish I could have a big do-over for.* His Boston accent was coming through thickly. I didn't realize how much his voice was trained for TV and movies until I was talking to him directly. And listening. Maybe he felt more comfortable with me. Maybe, I don't know this was all so weird.

That was the wrong relationship? You said earlier you fell in love with the wrong person.

Yeah, that's the one. He nodded.

"Aaarrrrrr!" I actually vocalized my noise of frustration. I was so frustrated and freaked out.

I ground my hands into my face and pulled on my skin as I dragged my fingers down. I sat in silence for a minute. Not really thinking, trying to blank my mind. Peter watched me.

Out loud I said, "I can't do this right now, I have a deadline."

Can I hang out?

"No, not right now. I'm having issues, as you can see, I'm having a conversation and there is no one here. And yet I'm having a conversation that no one else can hear." I think I was talking louder than necessary because I wanted to establish my own insanity.

I returned to my computer.

The blue lines of the sketch mocked me. Like I really had it in me to focus on this drawing. Focus or not, deadlines needed to be met.

I let out another roar of frustration the second Peter left. I felt completely alone.

A soft knock on my wall was followed by Holly peeking her head in tentatively. "You okay in here? You're making noises."

"Yeah, sorry about that, this kidney is giving me fits for some reason."

She walked farther into the cubicle. "You sure you're okay, you look..." She air drew a circle around her face indicating that mine looked off. My makeup was probably running from my leaking earlier.

"Oh," I grabbed a tissue. "Allergies or something. In the middle of this thing, I started leaking."

Holly looked at me from the corner of her eyes. "Emotional kidney is it?"

"Yeah. No, allergies probably got makeup in my eyes and they started watering like crazy. I should go wash my face." I followed her out, she returned to her cubicle, and I continued down the hall to the restroom to splash cold water on my face.

I didn't know what to do. Peter was really real. We were having really real dream sex. I tried to sweat out my freak attack at the gym. It felt good. I pushed it with the weights, by the time I was done, my muscles moved like limp noodles. I would be feeling it the next day.

Peter didn't come back that night. I owed him an apology. My head was going a million different directions, and I hadn't even extended him the courtesy of believing him. He was my lover had I clearly hadn't fully believed in him. He was dead, he wasn't happy about it, and I was being rude. At least I think I was. I had no idea what appropriate ghost interaction behavior was.

I started writing as soon as I got home. A dam had opened and words started flowing. My trust issues with Peter translated into trust issues for Johnny and everyone around him. I felt really good with the passage I had written. I realized I was still in my sweaty gym clothes when I finally got up from the computer. I went downstairs and made myself something quick for dinner. While it heated up I chowed on my homemade hummus and some chips. It was getting better each week I made it. By the time I had eaten and taken a shower I was exhausted. I fell asleep seconds after my head hit the pillow.

I lay on my side, propped up on my elbow. I admired Peter's handsome face. His hair was a tousled mess and splayed across his forehead. He had accepted my profuse apologies, and the makeup sex was mind-blowing. He lay back seemingly exhausted. The blond of his hair showed in stark contrast against his dark brows and his dark lashes. They looked black against his tan cheeks. Without touching him I trailed my finger millimeters off his skin. I followed the slope of his nose then I traced his lips.

"That tickles." His voice was a pleasant tenor rumble in his chest.

"I'm not touching you." I continued to visually outline his lips. He grabbed my hand away from his face and turned toward me.

"It still tickles." His eyes crinkled slightly at the corners as he grinned at me.

I lost my train of thought as I took in his expression. I wished he could look at me like that forever. I blinked, pulling back the thought I was supposed to tell him about. I trailed my finger into the soft hairs on his chest. I remembered what I was going to tell him. He wasn't going to like it.

"I'm going on a date tomorrow night with Holly again."

"No." It was more menacing in its quiet volume than had he roared. He grabbed my hand against his chest. "I don't want you seeing other men. I don't want you sleeping with anyone else."

"I know, I'm not going to have sex with anyone. But I need to keep up the pretense of being single. No one knows about you Pete, and I can't exactly tell people about you unless I want to end up locked up in a straitjacket."

He pulled me into his arms and rolled onto his back. Draped across his chest, I looked down into his eyes. "It's not going to mean anything, okay. Holly likes to date but doesn't like to go out alone with some guys. I don't blame her. I'm there for personal safety, nothing more."

"I still don't like it."

"You cannot like it all you want Peter, but that's how it's gonna be. I'd rather go out with you, but that's not possible."

He pet my shoulders, there really wasn't anything he could do or say. We were stuck. He was limited to the dream plane or being a voice in my head. He was tangible enough here. I needed to accept that our physical contact was limited. Other aspects of our relationship were pretty nice. The head talking thing made certain conversations easy to have, and he could hang out with me at work without anyone saying boo about it. But there was no physical contact while I was awake, and that pretty much sucked.

"I just wish I could see you and hold you when I'm awake," I confessed.

"I'm sorry Gil."

I wanted to tell him I loved him, but that wouldn't help our situation at all. I had once when we were just friends, but if I said it now. No, I couldn't. I loved him but it was beyond as friends. If I told him I loved him now I would only end up getting hurt worse. I lowered my head to his chest and hugged him fiercely. Peter rolled me and tucked me into the curve of his body. He held me against his chest.

One second I was asleep with Peter wrapped around me. The next I was awake and alone in bed. I cried at the injustice of it. It was going to be a long lonely day without Peter. I had no way to let him know I needed him by my side today, even if it was just his voice in my head.

I dragged my sorry carcass into work. I had made no effort and was barely dressed within the business-casual standards of our office. At least my jeans didn't have holes in them. There was not enough coffee in the world to fix my mood today. I promised to go on a date that I wasn't particularly interested in participating in. I didn't like anything in my wardrobe, and I certainly couldn't wear what I had on. And I wanted Peter.

Everything wrong in my life came down to that. I wanted Peter and I couldn't really have him. It felt like a stab in the gut with a flaming sword.

I cranked out my work. It wasn't particularly interesting, another info-graphic for the same group with the boring glands. This time it was needles, and the vials the pharmaceuticals came in. We didn't call them drugs at the university so we could differentiate between illicit substances and medicines. They were all drugs in my head, but it upset some people on the university's board that we worked with "drugs," so an institute-wide policy on nomenclature was in effect. I guess the expanded vocabulary didn't hurt, making most of us sound smarter than we actually were on a daily basis.

Holly popped her head into my cube. "Are you excited about tonight?"

I groaned at her.

"Oh no." She frowned looking at me. I was not wearing anything that could even remotely function as a work-to-evening outfit. "You feeling okay? You're still going out tonight?" She was worried. I didn't want to go, but I wasn't going to bail on her. I didn't want to let her down, she had too many people in her life do that to her. I wasn't going to be one of them.

"Bad David morning." She still accepted mourning my relationship with David as a reason for things to not be smooth in my life. What I wanted to say was bad Peter morning. I missed him hard.

"It'll be okay." She patted my shoulder.

"I know thanks. I'll change before we go. You don't mind swinging by my place to pick me up, do you?" I thought I could duck out a little early, run home, change, then have her swoop in and off we go.

"That will work." She nodded.

"Do I have to be sexy tonight or can I just be okay? Wondering if this mood doesn't lift."

"Okay is fine, I mean they think we are coming straight from the office. I wouldn't go with too sexy either way."

"Sounds good."

I spent the rest of the day barely focused on my work, and mostly focused on looking at Peter on the internet. I started with my favorite images. I tried to imagine his smiling face looking at me, and not some camera. I closed my eyes and tried to remember him from last night. His smile, his eyes, his hands. He did some amazing things with those hands and his lips.

I watched clips from his movies on YouTube. I found some outtake videos. He looked like he had been easy to work with, at least in the clips I saw. He always smiled, and if he messed up he would start cracking up, so would the crew. No one ever looked cranky on set.

Didn't Peter remember any of this? He seemed fairly bitter regarding the turn his career took but watching him work, he seemed to really enjoy himself. So did everyone else around him.

Sure he never made big budget movies and wasn't considered a major movie star, but he was in a lot of movies. He was a working actor. Wasn't that really the point?

I clicked over to the "We Love Peter Keith RIP" group to see if there was anything new and interesting I should look at. There had been a lot of activity since the anniversary of his death was coming up soon. There was a lot more fan art than I had seen before: the expected portrait, and some unexpected jewelry. There were also a lot of Peter Keith tattoos. Random quotes from his movie characters. A few *Trouble Trouble* quotes. His character Johnny was always saying "s'up now?" I didn't think of it exactly as tattoo fodder but to each their own. There were also quite a few portrait tattoos of him. Now I love Peter, but I do not want his face tattooed across my ass.

Some woman claiming to be his widow posted how she planned on starting a memorial blog and asked fans to send in stories. I followed the link. Currently, it only led to an under construction page for some future website.

I bookmarked the website. It might be worth checking out as a resource if I stalled out when it came to writing about Johnny Urban. Some fans posted links to articles that had been written about Peter since his death. I tagged them to come back and read later. They looked like they might be able to provide some character points for me to use as I morphed Peter Keith into Johnny Urban.

It was obsess on all things Peter day, but I also had to get some work done. I would have to postpone some of my research. Yes, I called it research instead of obsessive fangirling, which in reality it was.

I left the building like Elvis as soon as 4:45 hit. I snuck out a side door and hoped no one would see me. I quickly walked home. I secretly hoped Peter would be there. I hadn't spoken to him all day. He was probably off pouting because I had a date and I was going on it. I picked up a dress I had worn to work earlier in the week. A cerulean, black, and white color block mod A-line. It was properly rumpled to look like I had come from the office. I put on some make-up, something I had not done that morning. I scrunched product into my hair and put in a little headband. I looked properly cute for a date. I wished Peter could see me, and appreciate how well I cleaned up.

Holly did. She giggled when I confessed I picked the dress off the floor since it was the first thing I saw.

My date did not. Actually, he didn't appreciate anything. We were late. The restaurant was noisy. Our waitress kept messing up. The food was lousy. He complained about everything, and not in a way that could be mocked or ridiculed later for my enjoyment. No, he was a negative boring guy. He never got my name right, so I started calling him by different names. I don't think he even noticed. On the other hand, Holly's date was cute and very outgoing. He had a real dynamic personality. Holly spent the entire time giggling and smiling. At least one of us had a good time.

15

Hey Pete, I read some articles about you. Some guy named John Lambert is making a movie about you.

I sat in the middle of my bed, slowly tapping out the transcription of the handwritten notebooks. Peter lounged. It was a rare moment of domesticity for us. Not doing anything, but being in each other's presence. Well, Peter being in my presence, and me having his voice in my head keeping me company. In any case, I needed this. Peter had avoided me all day after my double date with Holly. I felt lonely and abandoned. I was the bad guy with him if I went so she didn't have to go out alone, and I was a bad guy with her if I stayed home because my ghost wanted me doing nothing instead. I couldn't win. Fortunately, he had come around. He knew the dates meant nothing to me, but everything to Holly. I needed to be around him right now.

He hadn't felt like working on the book, but I did. I took the advice of the crow and continued to work on my own. I hadn't told Trina about us yet, but I knew that would happen soon. I knew better than to ignore the counsel of a crow spirit. Crow spirits were supposed to be powerful and provide insight and wisdom.

Lambert? He sounded amused. *He produced and directed a bunch of the movies I made the past five years or so. He's a good guy. What else did it say?*

Nothing much, it was a recap of a press release. Just said filmmaker John Lambert was making a movie based on the life of his late friend Peter Keith. How many movies did you two make?

I think we made about ten, maybe twelve, movies together.

That's a lot of movies. I always thought it took at least two years to make a movie. Ten to twelve movies, that's practically a lifelong career right there. Clearly, I needed to research more about Peter's acting career. I also needed to find out more about this movie that was being made.

I returned to typing and Peter went back to whatever it was he was doing. I tried to close my eyes and look, but all I got was a sense of his presence, not an actual presence that I would see.

I continued to transcribe for hours. At some point, Peter faded off into the ether. I really should ask him someday where he got himself off to. Finishing a full notebook was a huge sense of accomplishment for me. I really needed to improve my typing skills. If I could touch type my writing process would be so much smoother. I wasn't planning on doing any kind of typing drills tonight. I couldn't face the repetitive skill-building exercises, even if they were disguised as video games.

I wanted to see if I could find anything more about this movie thing. I followed a few search links to articles that were really no more than what I had already read. I tried searching for a few different keyword combinations. I ended up finding that Peter's wife, Michelle Cruz-Keith, had, in fact, launched her blog, and John Lambert had posted as a guest blogger.

Reading Michelle's blog created mixed emotions for me. I knew all about this woman, yet I had never known anything about her. I was still a little mad at Peter for that. It wasn't fair of me I know. He had told me the truth all along, and somehow I convinced myself it was my imagination. What I thought I made up about Michelle Cole had been completely based on Michelle Cruz-Keith.

It was hard enough finding out her name was Michelle and that she was, in fact, a curvy Hispanic woman. But he really had picked her up at a bus stop on one rainy evening. The difference between Peter's Michelle Cruz-Keith and Johnny's Michelle Cole was the character I wrote did not get on the motorcycle and really didn't know who Johnny was. Peter's wife knew exactly who he was and apparently rode more than his motorcycle that night.

I stared numbly at the screen, not yet prepared to read the words that Michelle Cruz-Keith had written.

"It's been almost a year since dear, sweet Peter left this mortal coil. I can't begin to tell everyone how difficult it has been, and how much I appreciate all the outpouring of love I have received. Peter rests peacefully now, no longer in the chronic pain that plagued him in his last few years of life. Coming to grips this past year with my grief has been difficult, but I am ready to share my stories. I have asked friends and family of Peter's to also share their stories. I am extending this offer to you, his fans, and extended family of love that I know Peter always appreciated. If you have any stories of how Peter positively touched your life or a funny interaction with him, please do share. He may have left us for now, but his memory will be with us forever."

I was a sobbing mess by the time I finished reading the short entry paragraph. Peter really didn't understand how much he was missed. Somehow, somewhere along the lines, he got it into his thick skull that he had disappointed his fans, let them down, and that no one missed him.

I kept reading. There were several posts. The second was a painting of Peter from one of the mock-buster movies he starred in. The caption merely read: "fan art, thank you so much for sharing your love of Peter."

The entry after that was titled "Prankster Pete." It was written by his older brother, the one whom he felt estranged from.

"It was hard burying my baby brother. He wasn't that old. I always thought of him as being so strong and fit. But accidents can take anyone at any time. The past few years I don't think Peter thought of us as being particularly close. I know I didn't have him over for dinner, or for a beer, or to watch football as much as I should have. But to me, Peter was constantly in my life. One of his movies was almost always on one of the thousand cable channels we have these days. I swear if one of his cheeseball monster flicks wasn't on TV, there would be one on within a few days. I always watched his movies. So to me, it felt like I was seeing him, or hearing him all the time. But I realize now that's not the same as actually being there. He may have been a presence in my life, but I wasn't one in his. I will regret this for the rest of my life. Remorse, it sucks. Go be a presence in your loved one's lives.

Now, I'm supposed to be telling you about how Peter was always playing practical jokes. We didn't grow up surfing. But we picked it up as soon as our parents moved us out to California. Peter's absolutely favorite thing to do was mess with my board. He would gain my trust, then offer to wax it for me. But the little bastard wouldn't wax it, he would oil it, or glue sand on it.

If I was really lucky it was the oil. I'd carry my board out, then try to slide on and ride it out to the breakers. Keyword try.

I'd slide my torso onto the board and keep on going, right off the other side. A few times I managed to not slide off until I was trying to stand up. My feet would slip on the oil-slicked surface and off I'd go with a particularly ungraceful fall. Now I say that's lucky because the oil would clean off easily, and I'd only lose a day of good surfing. I'm ashamed to admit, he got away with oiling my board up more than once. I claim distraction by bikini in my defense. One time, I could have killed him. He glued sand or sandpaper to my board. Scrapped the hell out of my chest. He's lucky he used white glue, so it eventually cleaned off. Almost ruined a new board.

If you didn't keep a close eye on Peter he would get you some-how. I'm gonna miss that. No one pranked me like Peter."

I sniffled. Peter needed to see this. He thought people weren't mourning his death. He was so wrong. There were even more entries. A lot of fan art, clearly some pieces were reposted on the blog that had been posted in the "We Love Peter Keith RIP" group.

I continued to scroll and read. The last blog entry was written by the filmmaker John Lambert, the one who was reported to be making a movie about Peter's life. It read like a progress report. The screenplay was still being modified, actors were hired, production was underway, filming was scheduled to begin soon. A good looking young man, with a chiseled jaw named Liam James, was cast to be Peter. The only picture they had of him showed that he had dark brown hair, but he had the right eyes. Peter's eyes were important to his look, at least for me they were. Hair could be bleached.

I sat staring at my computer screen, the picture of Liam James dissolved into a rotating pattern of colored lights as my screen saver took over. This was going to change every-thing with Peter I could tell. These were the people who had been important to him, not me. I was some random person who was trying to help. I had never been an integral part of his life. The book wouldn't magically let him transition over. It would make his ghost feel better, maybe, but it wasn't going to help calm his spirit in anyway. Not like this blog, or the movie. I needed Peter to see this, but I also realized this was going to change the dynamic of our relationship.

I should be laughing at myself, calling what we had a relationship. It was a series of really hot wet dreams and very little else. I needed to get a grip on reality. I still had issues wrapping my head around his reality. It made me happy to think Peter liked me, and I mean really liked me. But I still had that lurking in the back of my mind this was just a fantasy I was making up.

It was and it wasn't. Peter was real, the relationship part was the fantasy. I always knew something would come up to burst my happy delusional bubble over Peter. I had a sinking feeling this was it.

The anniversary of Peter's death sort of snuck up on me. I knew it was fast approaching, but I didn't realize it was the day until I logged on to the online group and there was an incredibly handsome picture of him. It momentarily took my breath away. That's how he looked when he was with me, yet to the rest of the world, he was lost, gone. I allowed myself to be distracted with all the memorials. Mostly "We love you," and "Miss you" posts.

When Peter came to me that night, he made no mention of it. I didn't feel like I needed to remind him. I didn't think it was something he necessarily wanted to remember. We made love, which was more like some wild circus acrobatic stunt act. I learned to love that I could make as much noise as I wanted or needed to when we were together. Our dream zone was completely soundproof.

Completely sated, I folded Peter into my embrace. He was so much bigger than me, but I loved holding him. He would rest his head on my chest, his warm breath on my skin. I alternated between petting his hair and tracing patterns on his shoulder. His shoulders were freckled, minor skin damage from becoming a surfer when his family moved to California as a teenager.

"I died today Gil." I guess the significance of the day had not escaped him.

"I know, I wasn't sure if I should say anything. They don't really make cards to cover this situation." I tried to laugh. I was concerned about how well he was holding up. I couldn't see his face, just the back of his head, I had no visual gauge to his emotions.

"It sucks, but I met you. That's fucked up." He pushed up to look at me. "I had to die to find you." He shifted, pulling me into his embrace. I looked up at him. His gaze was soft as he drank in my face. His fingers softly traced along my jaw. "I never told you that Michelle and I were in the middle of getting a divorce, did I?"

"No, I think I thought you had already been divorced. Even though you never called her your ex, just your wife."

"Yeah, I guess technically she's my widow." He huffed.

"What's going on in that head of yours, Pete?" I tapped him on the forehead.

"I did things all wrong, and now I can't fix them. And somehow in the middle of all of this, there's you."

"Wrong person in the wrong place and the wrong time. I've always had impeccable timing that way," I said.

"No, right person, right place, wrong time. I should have

known you when I was alive." He traced my lips with his finger. I bit it gently.

"Peter Keith, you big phony. You never would have looked at me twice when you were alive."

"Probably not, but I should have. That's what I did wrong. So much stuff like that, I was such an ass. Do you think it's possible to become a better man after death?"

I shook my head, I didn't know.

"Regret weighs heavy on my mind tonight." He confessed.

"Maybe this is that whole afterlife penitence. You have to reflect on your life and regret the wrongs you did and realize what the better choices would have been. When you got to the next level you get to pass go, collect two hundred dollars. If you stayed an asshole after you died, then you're stuck until either you figure it out, or you score a get of jail free card."

"So do I get to pass go?" He shifted me under him and kneed my legs apart.

"I'm sure you're headed in the right direction." I wrapped my legs over his hips in invitation.

He slid into me smoothly. This time making love was gentle, caring. I felt he needed the succor and comfort of my arms, while earlier, he needed the distraction of the wild monkey sex acts.

When Peter didn't show up for a few days, I tried not to panic. He had taken himself over to the movie set, I kept telling myself. I had no idea. I preferred to think that rather than any of the alternatives my brain could come up with.

When I saw him again, I peppered his face with kisses. I

tried to get my hands into his shirt. My fingers seeking the soft ticklish flesh above his hip bone. He laughed and held me.

"You're in a frisky mood," he chuckled.

"I missed you." I kissed his grinning face.

"I don't think you ever missed the last guy this much."

"Who David? No, then again, I don't think I was addicted to him. I'm positively addicted to you, and I am desperate for a fix."

Peter obliged my physical needs. I was well satiated when he finished. "Will you be here when I wake up?" I purred into his chest as I lay draped across him.

"Hmmm," he hummed. It was neither positive nor negative.

"At least come see me at work?"

"I can do that." His voice was a tired rumble.

I fell asleep as his blanket. I woke up alone, as usual.

I counted the minutes of our time together. Peter hung out with me for three nights and two days before he disappeared again.

Hi, I sighed happily when I heard him in my head. *Where have you been off to?*

Nowhere. His answer was more of a grunt than actual words.

Surfing the dream plane? It seemed as good of a theory as any I had for where ever it was he went.

Something like that. Irritation radiated from his essence. I didn't need to see him to feel his agitation.

Are you okay? You aren't happy. Can I help?

Just let me be.

Easier said than done ghost man. I didn't want to let him be. I wanted to soothe his pain and hold him close. I wanted him home with me.

Do you just want to hang out? I'm almost done here. I wasn't really but nobody would mind if I ditched out of work a little bit early.

Whatever.

Will you come over tonight?

Can you just drop it, Gil? And poof he was gone.

"No, I can't just drop it, I thought you were my boyfriend. I haven't seen you in a few days, and I miss you. Sorry I was happy to have you around for a few miserable seconds," I rage whispered under my breath.

When Peter didn't show up for a few days again I let myself become distracted by work. I put all my focus into what I was doing as I did it. Same for my workouts. I focused all my intentions on my actions. It took some work, and it really only kept my mind from worrying for a few minutes at a time.

I constantly reminded myself to refocus. My brain kept switching, but I tried to force it to behave.

By forcing myself to focus, I actually was able to complete a few assignments on time. Of course, it all fell apart as soon as I got home, I couldn't focus on anything. I couldn't work on the story. I had a hard time even watching TV.

I went on an abysmal double date with Holly. I was twitchy and distracted. By the time it was over I couldn't get home fast enough, only to fidget and continue to be distracted. Nothing could hold my attention for more than a few minutes at a time.

Each time Peter came home to me I was ecstatic, and each time he left I became more depressed. I learned quickly, that if I wanted him to stick around I didn't ask where he had been. Clearly, it was very personal and very emotional for him. I suspected he was haunting the movie set. He would come back bristling and angry, or happy and carefree. Of course, I preferred happy and carefree Peter over brooding Peter. Happy Peter was more fun in bed.

I tried to dream of him. I wanted to dream about him if I couldn't actually have him around. It never worked. I would start consciously dreaming about him, but inevitably he would fade away and the dream would continue along some random tangent. A few times the dreams managed to morph into Johnny Urban, but only for a few moments before I would lose any connections to Peter at all.

I would have been happy with a mundane dream, it didn't need to be erotic. It just needed to be Pete. I longed for the days when his presence calmed my dreams. I wanted to go back to when his presence meant a happy surprise and not an indication of an impending miserable absence. I was having a hard time enjoying him when he was around. We bickered over stupid things. I was keenly aware that I would be feeling the pain of his absence soon every time he was with me.

My focus never fully returned. I tried to work on the book only to find myself staring at a blank white page with thin blue lines. If I tried to write, my mind would drift and I would think about how Peter's fingers felt as they caressed my cheek, or how warm his skin would be when I curled into his arms. I would be distracted by memories of how his breath felt on my neck or the sound of his laugh. If I remembered I was writing, I would discover I was still in front of a blank page. Usually, I forgot I was trying to write at all.

Work was painfully quiet, even with headphones and music. I missed the feeling of his voice in my head. Real sounds were harsh in my ears. I longed for the soothing tones of his voice.

Missing him felt like a gaping hole through my middle.

Each day he was gone, it grew like a black-hole consuming everything that got caught in its gravity well. I felt like I would fall into it, sucked in past its event horizon and crushed into a singularity of pain. But, no, I always traveled along the edge. Too strong to be completely consumed by it, but not strong enough to escape its pull.

Every time I saw Peter, I wanted to hold on to him. Things were changing between us. I wasn't sure if it actually changing on their own or if my paranoia was the driving force. I was in my favorite place, under him. I loved how his arms would block me in as he held himself up on his elbows. I wanted to keep him here, like this. His face so close to mine. It was strong and beautiful. I caressed his cheeks and traced his jawline. He was always clean shaven, sometimes he would have a mild scratch of whiskers.

He turned and grabbed my fingers with his teeth.

A giggle turned into a sigh as he started sucking on the fingers. It pulled sensations in other parts of my body. I closed my eyes and reveled in the feel of him. His weight, his skin. In the dream plane, he was smooth warm skin and hard muscles. I wished with everything I had that I could have this in my conscious reality. But as they say, if wishes were horses then beggars would ride. This beggar wanted to ride when she was awake.

Peter started biting me on the chin. A scrape of teeth. I raised my chin up, he shifted his bites to my exposed neck. A low growl escaped his throat. It was a low animalistic sexy sound. And he wondered why I wanted to make him into some were-beast. He was already a sexy animal, I wanted to amplify that for everyone who didn't get to experience this with him.

As he kissed down my neck, he shifted his arms away from encircling my head. One hand palmed a breast. The other breast was sucked into his hot, wet mouth. He must have sucked my air out with that action. I gasped. He could suck on that all night as far I was concerned. It felt so good. No, good wasn't strong enough of a word. He had skills that I appreciated greatly. The man could bring me to near orgasm simply by licking and playing with my breasts and nipples. Of course, my other body parts protested the neglect and lack of attention. I ran a leg up his and lifted my hips trying to rub against his erection.

He shifted his lower body out of my reach. I would have pouted if he wasn't distracting my upper half with his tongue. My lower half was protesting on its own, rubbing against his strong thigh, it wanted some of that tongue action.

I didn't realize how much I liked that tongue action until Peter and I started doing this. I mean, I appreciated the licks and sucks I had received in the past but Peter worshiped me with his tongue. My body would sing when he did his magic. Frequently, those sounds came out of my mouth. At least here I could scream and whimper and moan as my body reacted to his, without having to worry about the neighbors hearing.

I wound up tighter than a watch. I needed something to suck on. I pulled his hand away from my breast and sucked on his fingers. It wasn't enough. I pushed him off and rolled him over. He laughed knowing what to expect when I got like this. It didn't stop him from hissing, as I pulled him into my mouth. I was far from gentle or artistic with my fellatio skills. I pulled as much of him in as I could before I gagged, then I pulled on him like I was drinking from a large straw. I didn't start moving in a rhythmic up and down motion until I felt fingers slide along the folds to my core. My lower body was finally getting the attention it desired.

I focused more on the fingers on my body than what I was doing. Peter took this as his cue to reposition me. I was back on my back, and his tongue was doing its magic. He brought me to orgasm so delectably, and he could keep me reacting at that level until it was torture to continue.

After I felt like I had soared into the stratosphere, crashed, and burned on re-entry, he wrapped his arms over my head and looked down at me again.

His kisses tasted like sex, and his tongue was as magical in my mouth. I tried to wrap a leg over his hip, but I was limp, noodle legged. I barely had it in me to return thrusts when he plunged into me. The sensations his body delivered inspired me to participate, and I found muscles to move with. We moved together, synchronized thrust and counter-thrust. I started spasming around him again, then he released his orgasm.

Peter rolled onto his back, pulling me with him. I always ended up on top this way. I guess he didn't want to crush me. Of course, I didn't mind it at all when he would momentarily collapse and I could feel all of his relaxed weight on me. I rested my head against his chest and panted, well satiated and happy.

I didn't want to move, fortunately, I didn't need to. Peter pulled a blanket up to cover me.

"Sleep," he directed.

"Stay," I requested.

———

16

Peter wasn't there when I woke up. I knew he wouldn't be. He had been spending noticeably less time with me. I missed him. The gaping black-hole in my middle wasn't as big and intimidating as it had been a few times previously, but it was still there. He had been going off to other places ever since I met him, but there was something different now when he would come back to me, and it wasn't his quixotic mood swings.

He had pretty much stopped helping me with the story. I was on my own with it. I started seriously exploring the were-tiger aspect I had wanted to bring in the entire time. It added an extra dimension to Johnny Urban's character. It also gave me a whole lot more to work with. Johnny Urban, were-tiger, vigilante, pop-star, action hero, was a pretty interesting character. I could do so much with him. I could go back and rework how to deal with the fractured vertebra, and the whole recovery at home thing. That was Peter's need, I wasn't sure if that's what Johnny Urban needed.

Even if this were-tiger thing didn't work out for the Johnny Urban story, it gave me some interesting storylines I could bring into something else. I could easily utilize it for the graphic novels I had been wanting to do. I wasn't sure if it would mesh with the psychic alien comic I wanted to do. I didn't have to incorporate that into this existing idea. I could develop that as its own thing without Peter's help. In the meantime, I started exploring making Johnny Urban more exciting: action hero in the movies, and secret real-life super-hero, were-tiger. I know it's not what Peter wanted.

I also thought about changing Michelle Cole up a bit too. She was a little too sweet and pansy-assed. I mean I liked her, but she had no balls. She was there simply to love and support Johnny no matter what he did. That's what Peter had wanted: a sweet, loving, bit of a doormat woman. But Peter didn't seem to care anymore. The most character she really showed was when she first met Johnny and chewed out those Latino boys for yelling rude things at her. After reviewing the material I had written on her, I wouldn't be surprised if she was a virgin on their wedding night— hadn't written that scene yet. No, Michelle Cole needed a revamp. She needed some agency.

My ideas weren't meshing with words, I had them, and they tripped over my fingers as I tried to type. I put down the computer and picked up a notebook to see if writing longhand would help. It just made things worse. My writing started to look more and more like hieroglyphics before I realized I was trying to draw the words and not merely write them.

My doodles became distracted as I noticed I sketched out a pornographic sex scene. I recognized the actions as a reflection of what Peter and I had accomplished, but the figures weren't us. Well, the man was Peter, maybe a little broader through the chest and shoulders, but the woman was curvy with hips and boobs. I wouldn't have any problems illustrating an adult graphic novel, with all the sexy details. I'm sure that had something to do with my job, I constantly drew bodies. Bodies standing still, bodies in motion. Why not draw bodies having sex? I parked that idea in the back of my head.

I lost time doodling out thumbnails. After a few hours, I had sketched an outline I could now translate into words.

I couldn't see how I could tell Trina about me and Peter. I knew I should, she was my best friend. She would provide counsel regarding a new relationship. But this one was so different. I could never introduce her to my latest lover. No matter how much I thought she might like him, there was no way to introduce them. It was physically impossible.

I remembered the crow and how I needed to tell her, but I couldn't. To be honest, I felt like an idiot. I had let myself fall for him. A doomed relationship from the very first kiss, yet I was hip deep in it. Even though I knew better. And now the relationship was changing so much, I was afraid if I did tell her I would jinx everything and it would be over.

Now Peter had this movie about him being made, and I didn't see him as much. He wasn't talking in my head every day. I missed the sound of his voice. Times like now I hated him for being dead. I realize if he had never died in the first place I wouldn't have met him, wouldn't have gotten into this crazy situation. If he was still alive, he would be living his life, still taking drugs, maybe getting a divorce from Michelle. I would still be with David, slowly becoming more and more unhappy, blissfully unaware that he was two-timing me with that blond, who not only took my man but was also after my job. Or, we would have finally broken up.

We really had been heading that way, now that I look back at it all.

I sighed, not meeting Peter would mean no novel in the works, no realization that I had stories in me that wanted out, that I could tap into another aspect of my creativity. As much as I was pissed at him for taking off, I had a very singular experience in that I got to know him and find out about him in a way that just couldn't happen as an obsessed fan looking someone up on the internet.

I wish he hadn't died and he had been able to continue making movies. Maybe if he had been able to get away from his wife he would have been able to seek recovery from the drugs. Maybe he had needed more time to realize how appreciated he had been by those around him.

I didn't want to regret anything about Peter Keith, and that included not having full disclosure with Trina. Yet, I was not able to tell her. I could tell her anything and everything about him except for that one incredibly important fact. He was my lover on the dream plane, and my body recognized that on the conscious plane.

"You are awfully gloomy today, what's up?" She asked as we strolled through the new open-air mall. We made our way through the newly developed shopping center that was built to resemble a high-end shopping district in an affluent area. The difference between this tree-lined street and a real fancy neighborhood beyond the obvious planned aspect of this one was the parking garage located at the end of the "street." The shopping along this side of the mall was limited to extremely expensive and exclusive dress shops where the only things above a size twelve were the numbers on the price tags.

Window shopping was even mildly depressing. The sizes were so incredibly skewed. We did wander into a few of the shops, and skinny hipped, no boobed me would fit a large or an extra-large in the sizes they carried. I really wondered who the hell their clientele were. Even if it were possible for me to fit in anything these stores carried, I couldn't afford it.

Sophie sat tucked into her stroller and we headed to the far end of the block for lunch. I was not a slave to impending deadlines today, so I took a long lunch.

"Life seems heavy these days." I sighed.

"That doesn't sound good."

"I think Peter is on his way out. He's not been around so much lately, and I hate to admit it, I really miss having him around." I admitted part of it. I did miss him, now if I could figure out how to get my brain and mouth to cooperate to tell the rest of it.

"Any thoughts as to why?"

I pulled the large heavy door open, and she pushed Sophie into the foyer of the restaurant.

"They are making a movie about him." I began as we followed the hostess to a table. "This place is too pretentious, they'll mess up the food," I said looking around. They had white table cloths. I questioned our logic in bringing Sophie here when I saw there were a few other people who had toddlers in tow.

I continued to tell her what I knew about the production of the movie, including how cute I thought Liam James was.

"I suspect that's where he's been lately. It makes sense. I mean they are already in production, which means faster results. I didn't even get half of that story written, and I haven't really been working on writing lately, besides who knows if it will ever be published. I don't even know how to go about getting that done." I confessed.

"I wouldn't force it, Gil. The story will come to you as

you need it. And you've always known Peter's time here was only temporary. I know you like him and are friends, but you need to realize you are going to have to let him go at some point."

"I know, I know." I knew, I just didn't want to.

We ordered our food. It was overpriced for what it was. We had to ask the waitress twice to bring ketchup for Sophie. I wasn't as impressed with the restaurant as the restaurant was with itself.

"I wish I knew why he had picked me to begin with," I said. Trina and Sophie had their food. I waited for my hamburger to return. The first time they served it, it was practically raw. I had requested well done.

"I mean, I am glad to have gotten to know him. And I am sad to think it might be coming to an end, but why me?"

"Are you serious with the 'why me' whine?" Trina laughed at me.

"Not quite the 'why me' whine, but, yeah. Why me? I mean, I'm not somebody he knew. I wasn't a fan. I'm not a psychic. Why me?"

"You are incredibly tapped into the *Other*, Gil, so why not you?"

"What do you mean tapped into the *Other*?"

"I mean the metaphysical. Other planes of existence. You pay attention to dream messages. That's what I mean by *Other*. Look, Gil, you always seem to know when Sophie needs something just before she does. You think she's an incredibly well-behaved toddler."

"She is," I agreed.

"No, she isn't. Not around everyone at least. You seem to know what she's going to want before she can pitch a fit for it. You know when to hand her paper and pencil for drawing, you know when she needs more ketchup."

"That's because I'm around her so much, you do the same," I offered as an excuse.

"Half the time I haven't picked up on her signals, and you're already acting on them. I think it's because you are more open on a subconscious level than most people are. You've told me about the cats and the Thing. So why not a human spirit that's wandering?"

The waitress delivered my hamburger I made her wait as I cut into it. It appeared to be properly cooked this time. I put a few of my fries onto Sophie's plate and she began dipping them in ketchup.

"See what I mean?" Trina pointed to Sophie. "I thought she was done eating, but clearly not. You gave her food and she now doesn't have to whine while she figures out how to ask for more food. You have preemptively taken care of her need."

I really wasn't sure what to say. I always knew what to give Sophie, it seemed like the right thing to do, giving her more fries even though she had already eaten.

"I bet you had imaginary friends when you were a kid."

"Doesn't everybody?" I asked between bites.

"No." She shook her head. "Not everybody. I bet you can remember specific details about them too."

"Trina, stop creeping me out." She was right. I had had imaginary friends when I was a kid, and I did remember definite details about them. There was more than one. There were three to be exact. The one when I was about seven, she was a nice lady. Then there were two when I was in high school. One was a man who died in World War II. He had flown with the Royal Air Force. He was waiting for his wife to join him. The other one was a young musician. He hadn't been around much. Gerald, the pilot, had hung around for a bit while he was waiting. Our neighbor at the time had been an old lady who was originally from England. Gerald disappeared right around the time she died. I never made that connection before. My imaginary friends had always been nice, I always figured they were my hyperactive imagination.

"So I'm right?" She asked.

I nodded in confirmation. I needed to think about this some more. I never considered myself to be a conduit of *Other* energies as Trina called it. *Other* was a good title for something that couldn't quite be described. Right along the lines of me calling the grey swimming entity the Thing.

"I kind of wish I had kept Peter imaginary. If the internet didn't exist he would be, I never would have found confirming information validating his existence."

I was still confused as to what I was going to do with this relationship if I could call it that. I couldn't tell Trina. It wasn't that a lady doesn't kiss and tell, I've kissed and told Trina plenty. There was something in me still denying it, or more likely something in me recognizing it as incredibly stupid, and I was saving myself the cosmic 'told you so' when it all collapsed.

We left the restaurant and began our slow stroll back to her van in the parking structure. A flock of crows was hanging out in the street and on the sidewalk.

"Did you know a flock of crows is called a murder?" I asked as we made our way toward the birds. They looked like a gang of thugs strutting around, cocky and challenging.

"That's not random or anything," Trina remarked.

I thought it was very timely until I looked around and the crows were gone. Well if that wasn't some kind of cosmic hint. I guess the crows reminding me I needed to confess to Trina.

17

———

I doodled, trying to figure out what needed to happen in this story I wanted to finish and was not actually working. It happened sometimes. I knew I should have been organizing my supplies, or straightening up, but I wasn't. I felt twitchy and in no mood to work. I didn't really care, besides, I goofed off so rarely, no one was going to say anything about it.

I wandered over to Holly's cubicle. "Hey, let's go get some coffee. I need to get out of here."

"Sure, give me a second." Holly began shifting papers around on her desk.

"We need to get out here now. Leave it." I normally would wait, but I needed to get out. I had an odd sense of urgency to leave. We walked past Adam on our way out. I actually looped my arm through his and told him he needed to come with us. Fortunately, he didn't argue with me, but he looked at me like I was crazy. I've been getting used to being thought of as the crazy one at work, so that was nothing new.

I focused on heading to the coffee shop across the quad

when the earthquake made my legs feel like jelly. The rocking stopped after mere seconds. It wasn't a strong earthquake, big enough to shake nerves up and rattle windows. We looked at each other. I know my eyes felt like they completely bugged out. Adam and Holly had the same shocked expression.

"I guess coffees off then?" I laughed nervously.

Holly released a nervous, stress filled laugh.

"I should make sure everyone is okay," Adam said before he headed back inside.

I quickly texted both Mike and Trina making sure they were okay. I called and left a voice mail for my parents letting them know everything was fine here. Holly did the same. I really wanted that coffee, something hot to calm my nerves was sorely needed now. Holly walked with me over to the campus coffee shop. Fortunately, they had only been rattled a bit and were still serving.

We walked back to our office, anticipating an aftershock. After we stepped into the building my ears popped.

"Did you feel that?" Holly asked.

"Yeah, aftershock." She nodded.

Back in the department, everyone was chattering nervously. Holly's cubicle was covered in small bits of glass. The light panel in the ceiling directly over her chair had been shaken loose. I had always thought those panels were made of plastic. Apparently, some really old ones were still glass. A few ceiling tiles had shifted, the only other ones to have fallen out were in Adam's office, and his entire ceiling had collapsed. No other damage was reported.

We stood looking in shock at Holly's cubicle. She threw her arms around me and squeezed.

"You saved me, Gillian!"

"I ah, whoa." I breathed deeply. I had insisted she leave

with me. Maybe Trina was right, maybe I was tapped into some *Other* force.

A few of us started helping Holly pick up glass bits. It appeared, by the way the glass had shattered that it was safety glass, which certainly made cleaning up easier. Holly told everyone how I had saved her by insisting she leaves immediately. And that I saved Adam too since I had literally dragged him outside with us.

I kept saying it was only a really weird coincidence, but honestly, I wasn't convinced. I needed to freak out. I took a few deep cleansing breaths and tried to calm myself before I started flapping my hands and crying. I needed Peter. I needed big strong arms surrounding me, and warm hands patting my hair, soothing me.

The next time I saw Trina I complained of just that, no Peter when I needed him. "My imaginary friend is letting me down." I toyed with the straw in my milkshake. I pulled it out and licked the thick ice creamy goodness from the straw before dunking it back down into the glass. The shake was entirely too thick to drink through a straw. Licking the shaft of the straw only deepened my depression, it was the only shaft I had the opportunity to lick for weeks, and for the foreseeable future.

I missed Peter.

"I don't know why you keep saying things like that. He's not something you made up. How else do you explain that Sophie could see him? Hmm?" Trina looked at me with her 'don't be a dumb-ass' expression. "Explain to me how if Peter is your imagination you were able to figure out David was cheating on you with that blonde?"

"You really think he's real and I'm not going crazy?" I countered.

"You've got something special going on with him, but you have got to be careful not to get carried away."

"Carried away?" I already was.

Sophie was occupied with ketchup, eating it with her fingers. Trina sat dissecting onion rings and giving Sophie the fried batter coating. We were comfortably ensconced in our lunch routine at the Soda Shoppe.

"I know you, Gil, you're going to get too invested in this guy, and you're going to get hurt."

"I set up boundaries early on." I didn't lie. I had. I also completely tossed those boundaries out once David was no longer in the picture.

"It's not going to stop you from developing strong feelings for him. He's very much real and flawed, and you're spending a whole lot of time alone with him."

I brushed off her comment. Trina was right, but right now she didn't need to know that.

"You should start dating again. And I mean really dating, not that go out with Holly thing you've been doing. But really date."

"I'm not ready for that. David really hurt me. I'm okay not dating for a bit." Now I was lying. I didn't want to date. It wasn't David that had hurt me. It was Peter who was ripping my heart out.

"Okay fine, don't date. But do something other than hiding in your room with Peter." She almost pleaded. She was more sensible than me.

"But we're working on this project," I whined.

"Have you made progress? You haven't shown me anything to read for ages."

"Well," I paused, "we've been having issues with that. I want the story to develop and go one way, and he really insists it take a different direction. He wants to make it too much biographical. I'm not comfortable with that. In order for me to do that properly, I should be interviewing other people and doing research. I mean I get he's telling me stuff, but how do I make it authentic otherwise?

"Besides, he's really not around as much anymore." I felt the hurt feelings in my own voice.

"What do you mean?" Trina asked.

"Ever since he found out that guy was making a movie about him, he's not just around as much. I think he's finally starting to realize that he had a big fan base out there. He might not have liked the movies he made, but his fans certainly did." I didn't tell her Peter and I were arguing whenever he was around. Stupid petty disagreements.

Unfortunately, I recognized that we were on a relationship burn-out trajectory. At first, he visited two to three times a week. Quickly it became every day. Every glorious day of having him in my head during the day, and in my bed at night. Then it began fading, once or twice a week if that much. He stayed away longer and longer each time. It's been over two weeks since the last time I saw him.

It physically hurt, and it hurt my feelings. I felt like I was being cast aside for something better. I filled a gap and was useful for a time. But something happened, something changed. I was no longer useful to Peter, and he didn't bother with me anymore.

It hurt because I had trusted him, and he was proving to be an opportunistic jerk. He may have thought he wanted to be different, but his afterlife actions we really showing how he had been alive. In reality, he never would have known what to do with a woman like the Michelle I wrote about— kind, loving, understanding, and supportive. No, he got the Michelle he deserved. Michelle Cruz-Keith—cunning, manipulative, opportunistic.

I wanted to blame all my unhappiness on missing him. I felt used. It wasn't all merely missing Peter, I felt like a chump.

"It might be easier if he was imaginary. Then all of this would be in my head, and I could seek medical help. Maybe they could give me a little blue pill to make me not hear him, and forget everything?"

"Sounds more like relationship problems, than a misunderstanding between friends."

I stared out the window as Trina made her painfully keen observation. The day was bright and sunny. And then it wasn't. The sky darkened as a mass of black birds, the likes that haven't even appeared in a horror movie, flew past the restaurant window. Crows.

Well, that was one strong reminder of what I needed to do. I didn't need to look around to see if anyone else had witnessed the mass of birds, they hadn't. That rush of crows was all for me. I blinked and the sky was clear again.

"It is relationship problems. I got involved with him, and not just working on the project."

Trina looked at me, her face neutral. I couldn't tell what she was thinking, probably practicing a non-judgmental expression while judging me harshly.

"I know, stupid move." I began my explanation. "We've been together since after David. I wouldn't touch him at all while I was with David. I didn't cheat. Peter waited for me to be over David."

Trina didn't say anything. I think she wanted to but she only nodded.

"We stopped working on the book a while ago. There didn't seem to be much point for a while. I've tried working on it on my own. But I'm not sure if it's ever going to happen at this point." That wasn't a lie, I had no idea if I was going to be able to get this novel to work.

I stopped talking. I started biting my thumbnail. I needed her to say something.

She tilted her head to the side, scrunched her eyebrows together and asked, "How?"

I laughed. I expected to be chewed out for being so dumb. I didn't expect her to ask how I managed to have a relationship with Peter.

"I can touch him in dreams, and he can control the dreamscape," I explained.

"So you two actually?" She was making hand motions, clearly unable to find words she could use around Sophie.

"Yes, we actually." I know I blushed. "And he's really freaking good at it." I had to pause. A profound sadness washed over me. I looked out the window, trying to will my tears away. It didn't work. I blinked trying to clear my eyes. "And that's why this sucks so much. He's not just moving on, I'm being cast aside like used goods."

"Oh honey, I'm so sorry. You really like him, huh?"

I nodded. I wiped my nose. "I like him better than I liked David. I miss him." My bottom lip quivered. I was a mess. Crying over a boy while drinking milkshakes, it was like I was in high school or something.

"I'm sorry," I sniffed, "I didn't tell you earlier. I've known it was a no-win situation and that I shouldn't have gotten involved from the beginning. I know I was setting myself up for a broken heart, but I couldn't help myself. And now here I am, and my heart is breaking. I'm not even all that mad at him, I miss him. I'm being dumped by a ghost. At least it's not for another woman." I laughed.

Trina ended up paying for my lunch out of pity. I should cry at lunch more often.

~

Trina had been right, I need to change things up. Hiding in my room all weekend alone wouldn't bring Peter around any faster. I needed my muse, clearly, he had other things to do with his time. No Peter to distract me. Mike was off on some wild, sex-filled weekend that I wouldn't hear about until he got back on Tuesday. Trina was never available on weekends. Holly had plans. I didn't have a large pool of friends to do things with. I tended to go for quality over quantity. But that meant I was left on my own, and I wanted to tackle this Johnny Urban thing.

Maybe if I worked in a different environment the creative juices would flow. I was a professional artist, I could not afford to wait for inspiration to strike. I had deadlines and drawings needed to be done. Why should writing be any different? What I needed was to establish a schedule, give myself a deadline; demand a certain word count per day or week.

The writers on TV and in the movies always worked at hippy coffee shops. I didn't exactly have one of those around, but I did have access to the student coffee shop across the quad from my office. There were always students on laptops, I would fit right in. Hell, half the people I met on campus thought I was a student anyway.

With laptop and notebook in hand, I found a table to set up at by the big window. I ordered a Frappuccino and sat down to work. My fingers rested on the keyboard but didn't move. I watched campus through the big picture window as if it were a TV. I saw a student with a particularly good outfit and thought that would look cute on Michelle. I started to describe what I saw. My words were lame, but I wanted to get that idea down on paper.

I flipped open my notebook that was already filling up with more sketches than words and jotted down a sketch of the outfit. I went back to staring out the window but my fingers kept moving. A single crow flew past.

"Oh no, not you again," I whispered.

When I looked down at my notebook, I had doodled out a crow. Yeah, I got the hint. I should be drawing this thing, not writing it. Why not make Johnny Urban a graphic novel? This was clearly my project now. Peter had fucked off to who knows where. He never wanted the story to do much more than be him having sex with Michelle and making her pregnant. She got pregnant every time they had sex, even if she was pregnant already.

Well, if I was going to do this thing, I was going to do it right. I needed characters, I needed more than just Johnny banging Michelle. I needed a plot, I needed action. I had ideas tucked away, Johnny Urban was going to be a were-tiger, Peter be damned.

I left the cafe and grabbed a sketch book from my office before heading to the mall. I wanted to make some character sketches. See if I could find some inspiration models for some characters I had created with words, and for characters I hadn't yet invented.

Johnny was easy: tall, brawny, blond. Michelle was also easy: super curvy, Hispanic, long flowing brown hair, big lips, bigger eyes. But other characters I had no idea what they should look like. I wasn't going to do character development on campus because of the lack of variety. Students seemed to fit into a limited set of looks. Girls wore oversized shirts, leggings, infinity scarves, and Ugg boots. Boys wore skinny jeans, blazers and infinity scarves. Then there was the third style group that consisted of boys and girls in jeans and T-shirts and chucks. There did not seem to be the wide variety of body types and styles on campus as I could find at the mall. I think a lot had to do with students on campus being from a narrow age range and similar financial backgrounds. The mall offered a larger range and variety of socioeconomic styles.

I had to wander up and down a bit before I found an open bench on which to park myself so I could work. I wanted to stay out of the food court, simply because not everyone went through there, and I wanted as much variety as I could access. I began sketching frantically, getting in as many details as I could in my limited time observing people as they walked past me.

I started sketching as much of each person as I could. I would pick someone walking slowly toward me, so I had some time to get as much visual detail in as I could. This wasn't working nearly as well as I had hoped. I couldn't sketch an entire person at once, not enough time. I began breaking the sketches into groups: body types, shapes of faces, clothing styles, haircuts.

I easily spent an hour sketching out tattoo ideas specifically. There were so many options, locations, and styles for tattoos. A tattoo was a great identifying feature for a bad guy, especially if the situation was such that the viewer didn't see his face right away, but did see his arm, or leg. I was toying with the idea of giving Johnny one. It wasn't the fact that Peter didn't have any tattoos that caused me to hesitate, the constant repetitive rendering of it caused me to hesitate. I realized I could place the tattoo across his chest, or on his back so that it would be covered with clothes most of the time. It would only be exposed when his clothes were off. Of course giving him a big tattoo would give Michelle Cole an excuse to touch him. It needed to be a tiger.

I knew I would give Michelle a tattoo. I had pretty much

decided she was going to have a thing for tigers, so she was going to have a tiger tattoo. Maybe it would match Johnny's tattoo if I gave him one. There was no way I could go with meek office assistant for her anymore, now she needed something fierce, intrinsically strong. Zookeeper or circus performer kept trying to make space in my head. They both had strong points in favor of the concepts. The zookeeper could have a history of working with big animals in the field, Africa or India. So zookeeper Michelle would be adventurous and know how to handle herself in exotic locations. Circus performer Michelle would be super agile, having started as a trapeze artist. She would know how to deal with people, and would have questionable connections practically everywhere she went.

Suddenly, Michelle was very noisy in my head as if she finally found her voice to tell me things. I wasn't sure of her job, but I knew exactly how Michelle would find out Johnny was a were-tiger. Confronted by bad guys, with no way out. Eminent death type situation, until a large tiger leaps into the fray, Michelle takes the opportunity to escape. Being familiar enough with large cats, she knows she has a limited window of opportunity to escape while the cat is occupied with the bad guys before it turns on her. An enraged tiger is not an animal to try to reason with. She'll have a thought bubble including information on a tiger's jumping range, and how she needs to get distance and obstacles between her and the beast. I'd have to research that.

I could picture the first panel of the scene, a bird's eye view of Michelle running into an alley, a typical alley with pallets and boxes and a dumpster. The buildings on either side would have metal fire escapes. The next panel would be a back view of Michelle as she stops. Confronted by a brick wall, the alley is a dead end. She turns and sees the silhouette of the large cat at the opening of the alley. In a series of small panels, I would show what Michelle sees as she assesses her situation, boxes and a pallet leaning against a brick wall, opposite a dumpster under a fire escape ladder. The action would be tricky to illustrate, I would have to show her completing multiple actions in one frame. I wanted to show her using the boxes and pallet to run up the wall parkour fashion, that free-running, gymnastic combination that's so popular in foot chase scenes in action movies. She would use the wall to launch herself across the alley onto the dumpster and leap up to the fire escape. She would then climb up several stories before leaping across the alley to a balcony.

When she looks down, a very nude Johnny Urban would be standing with his hands on his hips laughing at himself over her escape. He would say something like, "Damn woman, here I thought you needed my help, clearly you can take care of yourself."

She would jump down, landing in a crouch before him. For a moment she would be the one to look like the dangerous beast, glowing eyes and hair fanned out around her. A metaphor for how Johnny sees her. She's beautiful, yet dangerous to him on an emotional level. He would comment on her ability to jump, it would have to be snide, a back-handed comment. He would step up to her, wrapping his arms around her hips. And as he leans in for a kiss, she slaps him across the face, hard.

Yeah, I could completely picture the entire exchange. I liked this version of Michelle Cole much better. Nothing wimpy about her. And she wanted to have a domestic side and be a baker. She wouldn't be a glorified housekeeper, no she would be equal, an integral part of Johnny Urban's ability to be a hero. The doodles and thumbnails I sketched made sense to me. The next step would be to actually draw it so that other people could see what I saw inside my head.

I went back to creating model studies of the people at the mall. I started making character pages for myself, taking some of the more distinctive sketches and fleshing them out a bit more. I had the sketch of the character on the left side of the page, and then I added descriptive words next to the drawing. I included things like hair color, height, accent, and what kind of person this character would be.

You've been at this for hours. Peter's voice was a chuckle in my head. I had forgotten he could find me at this mall, after all it had some sort of metaphysical energy rift through it.

Oh my God Peter, how long have you been here? I hated that I couldn't hear him sneak up on me. I also hated thinking he's been here and I had been ignoring him.

For a while, you've been so engrossed. I sat here watching you. He practically purred. He sounded happy and content.

I've missed you. I started packing my things up. I wanted to talk to him, and I wanted to be with him. Talking, I could do in the mall, be with, I could not. I had to be asleep for that to work.

Don't stop on my account. He said. *You can keep drawing, you looked very serene. It's why I didn't disturb you.*

But I haven't seen you for days. I knew I whined.

I know. I wanted to say hi. I'll be back again soon.

You're not staying? I asked. I was hurt.

I'll be back in a few days, don't fuss.

Don't fuss? He told me not to fuss. I hadn't seen him in days and he treated me like I was acting crazy and possessive. He hadn't seen crazy and possessive yet.

Don't treat me like I'm acting possessive and clingy. I simply told you I missed you. I clenched my jaw, I even sounded as if

I was hissing through my teeth. I fully resented him at that moment.

I said I'll be back, you need to relax, Gilligan.

I felt like the top of my head was about to erupt like Krakatoa. He was being a complete ass. And I felt like kicking the hornet's nest.

Well, you just go and have a good time, but try to only come back while I'm at work. I think I'm going to start sleeping with the guy I went out with last week. I really don't want an audience. It was all a lie, but he wanted to treat me like a crazy person, then I was going stick him where I knew it hurt.

My sketchbook flew off the bench. I stared at it. Peter's ability to move the physical was so unpredictable. I could hear him growling. I had pissed him off. I smiled at that little triumph.

Don't like that idea much do you? I smirked.

Gillian, I told you I don't want you sleeping with anyone else. He growled.

So you want me to become a nun or something? Cause I haven't been sleeping with anybody, including you. I yelled in my head. Treat me like some crazy bitch, and I'll give you crazy bitch. Most people don't like it when I lose my cool. Redheads have earned their fiery temper reputation. I was no exception. I was hurt and angry. Not a good combination. *You want me to act like your girlfriend, and have some sort of exclusive relationship with you then I think you need to suck it up and realize I'm not going to sit around at home twiddling my thumbs waiting for you.*

That's not what I meant, Gil. His tone was softer, I could sense the back peddling. At least he knew now was the time to start backing off.

No. You meant that you want me to be available when you want me. I went through that bullshit with David, and you're trying it now. Uh uh. I'm not playing like that Peter. If you want me then you need to want me. And you need to let me know that you want me. Disappearing for days at a time, then stopping by to say, 'hi oh don't get mad that I keep disappearing on you,' isn't gonna cut it. It's not like I can call you to see if you're okay. I don't make plans thinking you might come home, then you don't. And knowing you, if I do make plans, you'll get all pissed off that I'm not available for you. Then you tell me to not fuss? Fuck that. I waited for him to respond. I continue to pack my things. I couldn't see him at all, not even if I closed my eyes. At first, I thought he might have absconded while I was chewing him out, then he spoke.

I'm sorry, Gil. His voice was soft.

I'm going home, I expect you to be there. I was not going to fuss. I was in bitch mode and told him what I wanted.

He was there when I got home. I stomped all the way into my room.

"Do it," I said out loud, as I lay down, expecting him to pull me into sleep. He did.

We had angry sex. It was aggressive and unforgiving, and it felt so much better than yelling did or hitting would. I turned into a mewling clingy mess afterward. I had missed him so much, and I told him so.

"This is something I need to be doing," he explained.

"I get that, but you could have told me. Don't just show up for a drive-by 'hi there see you later.' Especially after you've been off for days." I felt like I should have told him that I loved him. Like that would be the leverage I needed to keep him with me. But it wasn't and I didn't.

"I need to go. I will be back for you." He stroked the side of my face. I watched him get dressed then walk out of my room. I stared at the door and willed him to walk back through it. I had never actually been interested in what was on the other side of that door until now. I got out of bed and opened the door. I fell forward into a swirl of color that morphed into my normal level of strange and weird dreams.

I woke up. My first thought was, well that's what's behind the door, more dreams. It was late, but I wasn't tired enough to go back to sleep for the night. I ended getting up, making some ramen, and watching TV movies into the early morning. My emotions were too numb to really process what was happening between Peter and myself.

Peter came back the next day. It was nice. He sat on a stool at the counter while I did my Sunday cooking and food prep. He didn't really talk about anything in particular. I enjoyed being with him. But it was different. It wasn't relaxed and casual. Our conversation was stilted and forced.

I felt like he was here out of a sense of obligation and not because he really wanted to be with me. He wasn't flirty, and he didn't try to look down my shirt. I wanted him here because I was being selfish, and I knew he would disappear again soon. I had no idea if it would be for days or weeks this time. The closer it got to the reported release date of the movie the longer Peter was gone.

I put my knife down. I didn't want to be chopping peppers and onions. I wanted to touch Peter. I was more in a mood for cuddling, but I wouldn't turn down more sex.

I have an idea, let me finish this then we can go upstairs. I suggested.

Peter huffed, it wasn't a positive or a negative sound. I really couldn't tell if he wanted to be with me. I know if he had been there and I could have touched him, I would have put down my knife right then, grabbed his hand and dragged him upstairs. Too many would haves and could haves.

I finished the onions after the peppers, then I washed

up. I wasn't in the mood to make salsa or hummus, even though I had purchased to ingredients to do so. Maybe I would later.

"Come on," I said out loud before I headed upstairs.

I curled up on my bed and waited to wake on the dream plane.

"What do you want from me, Gil?" Peter asked.

I want your future. I want your children. I want your love. I want to know you won't ever leave me. There were so many things I wanted from Peter that I could never tell him. I settled for, "I want you to hold me."

He pulled me into his embrace. He felt warm and comfortable. I wanted to cuddle and be held, but I was bad at it. He was so close and smelled so good. I couldn't help myself. I began caressing his chest and licking at his arms where my head rested against them.

He chuckled, "I'm not going to only hold you if you keep that up."

"Okay, I'll be good." I snuggled in and for a few minutes, I rested against him. It probably wasn't very long before I groped him again.

Peter chuckled again and removed my hands from his crotch. I snaked my hands under his shirt and tickled along the side of his ribs. He shook his head, sighing exasperatedly with me. But he smiled. I petted his crotch again, I could feel his cock growing under the fabric of his pants.

"Keep that up, and I'll have to take action, and not be limited to snuggling." He laughed.

"Promise?" I asked as I continued to massage him through his clothes.

Peter flipped me around and clamped down on my breast with his mouth. He sucked at me through my clothes. I smiled, I was getting what my body wanted, to be touched excessively by him. There was a small part of my brain that was sad. It felt that I had to do this as much as possible before he left me for good.

He pulled my clothes from me and started kissing me possessively. I was too caught up in the touching to focus on getting his clothes off right away. There was something incredibly sexy about being naked, and being kissed and caressed while he was fully clothed. He pulled away long enough to remove his clothes. I was on him, touching his skin, feeling the hairs on his chest tickling my fingertips. I started running my hands over all of him, down his legs, across his abs. I looked at him with as much love as I felt. I wondered if he could see it in my face.

He kissed me again. He shifted us so he was back on top. I liked him up there. He felt so firm and strong. He had the type of body that would be hard to follow up with another soft-bodied lover. If I ever get over him when this ends I'm going to have to start fraternizing with some of those young men in the fitness center. I'll be good and make sure they are either seniors or graduate students.

I chuckled at my train of thought. How could I think of anything other than the man above me? I was too distracted with other thoughts when I should be properly distracted by him. I slid my leg up his, then lost any and all thought beyond how his body felt against mine.

I fell asleep in his arms in post coital bliss. He left while I slept. When I woke up I knew it would be a very long time before I saw him again, if ever. At least he hadn't left me after an argument.

18

I spent the next few weeks bouncing between cross, cranky, and crying uncontrollably—I recovered faster from breaking up with David. Then again, that relationship had closure, this one had nothing. We didn't have a last argument or a "see ya later." I had nothing. Peter was gone. He abandoned me.

Had he moved on? I didn't know. But he was dead as far as my heart cared. Not dead to me, but from me. His death finally took him away from me, and it hurt with every fiber of my being. But I couldn't mourn the loss publicly. Peter hadn't left me for another woman. No, he left me because of his life.

The first week of my abandonment, I continued to read Michelle's blog almost daily. It was updated constantly, so there was always new information. John Lambert frequently posted regarding the movie.

The second week, when I figured he wasn't coming back, I was pissed. A few days later, the crying started. At least with David, I had been distracted by Peter so I didn't break down at work over the break up. This time, I had no distractions, and try as I might to be cool and collected, I failed.

I frequently worked through tears. I was not a pleasant sight. My nose was red from blowing it, and my eyes were constantly rimmed in red as well. I couldn't wear makeup because I would cry it off before lunch time.

Dressing was hit or miss. The days I wore dresses were the days I looked like I had thought about clothes. Actually, dresses were easy, one piece, no waistband, I looked put together. I found myself wearing more dresses than normal, just because of the ease of them. When I branched out and wore skirts or tried to put together an ensemble, I tended to look like a bag lady or a three year old learning how to dress. I ignored rules for blending patterns and colors. I clashed or I wore only black.

I missed an important deadline for the first time ever. Even when I had been seriously ill and missed a week of work, I hadn't miss deadlines. I had completely forgotten to finish the illustration. I really didn't care either. Adam was more upset with me because I just stared at him, a numb lump, as he confronted me over the missing work than he was over missing the deadline. I couldn't bring myself to care. I had to work over the weekend to finish it for a late delivery on Monday. It had been a very quiet weekend. The last time I had to work overtime, Peter had hung out with me. He had kept my brain entertained. I turned in tear stained sketches, and a final digital file. Thank goodness it wasn't a water color or colored pencil job. I would have ruined it.

"This is just a delayed reaction to breaking up with David. I'm convinced of it," Holly said. "You didn't see him with Jenny, did you? That must have been like reopening the wound."

I never told her about Peter, so it was easier for her to continue thinking it was me missing David. Part of me really did want to correct her. I didn't want her thinking David had affected me so profoundly. But, how would I explain that missing the living guy was no big deal, yet the phantom of someone I never met had disappeared from my life, and my body felt like it was being torn in half? He made promises to me he had not kept. I had trusted him, and he left me hanging. That hurt almost as bad as wondering if he realized how much I had fallen in love with him.

The tears finally dried, and I realized I had things to take care of. Johnny Urban hadn't left me, Peter had. And the voice of Michelle was getting louder in my head. I called her the Michelle Muse. With no Peter around, she took on a very strong voice, and had opinions on how women needed to be portrayed.

Together, since it felt like she guided me, we worked on Michelle's look. She wasn't another Peter, who was a tangible voice in my head when he wasn't in my dreams. No, Michelle was less actual voice and more an inkling of an idea that would grow and swell, and develop on its own. She was a hint, a whisper, a correction—a very opinionated correction.

The character sketch of Michelle Cole originally had her with large breasts, a tiny waist, and full round hips wearing form fitting, bellybutton revealing clothes. That's not what she wanted, needed, or thought she would wear. Michelle Cole was a bad-ass, who just happened to be dealt a good set of genetics.

Hour glass figure, yes, but she wore practical clothes for her work with big cats. Her pants came with lots of pockets and were loose so she could move. I was originally inclined to create a look that fit the comic styles I grew up with, not realizing I was contributing to unintentional misogynistic over-sexualization of female characters. The Michelle Muse guided my hand away from all of that.

The final Michelle sketch wore cargo pants, sturdy work boots, and a T-shirt that hung loose, or was tucked in, and frequently had a riding crop tucked into her belt. Nothing skimmed, nothing pulled, and nothing was so tight to look like a seam was headed up her butt crack. And her T-shirts always had tigers on the front, always. Her hair was big and wild, and more uncontrollable than the big cats she worked with. She was still sexy as hell, but now, she was sexy and comfortable.

With my new muse, and the need to prove to myself, and to Peter that I could do it, I created a work schedule. As I began story boarding, I realized I needed help, and I just happened to know professionals in the field who could help me. I confessed to Holly that I had been writing, but the words weren't working anymore, however, the pictures were, and now, I needed help producing a graphic novel.

One long evening over margaritas and nachos at the condo, she and Mike helped me to figure out a production schedule. We used a long roll of butcher paper and starting at the end with delivery day, we plotted backward, mapping out a timeline that took into account my ideal work schedule. Once that was complete, we opened a calendar, and working in the opposite direction, assigned dates to all the milestones that I needed to reach. We also mapped out exactly how many graphic novels it would take to complete the story I wanted to tell.

～

I stared at the blank page, my hand poised to draw. I knew what was about to start flowing from my fingers. I had the entire passage in my head. It had built momentum all day long. Actually, it felt like Michelle pestered me to produce. She was almost as loud of a voice in my head as Peter. Almost.

I didn't even have to focus on it and the next thing I knew, I had a full blown scene in my head demanding to get out. The Michelle Muse made sure I saw things from the feminist perspective. She conveyed plot and action almost as prolifically as Peter did for Johnny. But, she focused more on the sentimental parts of the story, the emotional factors.

And she wanted me to tell the story of their wedding. This would take an entire edition to my series to tell. She tossed all kinds of pictures into my head about an ornate Catholic ceremony. She pretty much had tunnel vision the entire time, and could only see Johnny. To her, he looked like an angel, and she would have sworn a heavenly glow surrounded him. She could actually see his aura, and it radiated with love and happiness. Through the Michelle Muse's eyes, I could see Johnny in a classic black tuxedo, starched white shirt, and a black bow tie. Nothing fancy, but he looked so beautiful and sexy—and he was hers.

Despite all the physical discomforts and stresses, she felt like she floated through the day. Her face hurt from all the smiling. Michelle breezed over the reception and was eager to get to the honeymoon. It wasn't so much that Michelle was hot to get Johnny in bed, it was the importance of them being married, and all the emotion it conveyed.

I worked to get the ideas on paper, in a combination of words and pictures. I grabbed my good markers, and began color sketches of the interior of the church as I saw it through her eyes. There was wainscoting of redwood panels, and then tiles or frescos painted directly onto the walls of religious symbols. The ceiling arched high into peaked vaults. Lit candles glowed golden and warm. I clearly needed to do some research on the interiors of Mexican Catholic churches. The only one I could remember ever being in had left the impression of slate gray and blues, not red—but she insisted on red. Everything was red while she and Johnny wore black and white.

Next, I sketched out her wedding dress. Michelle hated the rustling noise her cumbersome gown made. She wondered how anyone felt like a princess in such a heavy monstrosity. The veil made her nose itch. These were all sensory inputs I could not draw. There would have to be lots of thought bubbles.

The wedding dress was lined up the back with a million tiny buttons. I made a side sketch to illustrate Johnny fumbling with and cursing all of the buttons trying to undress her.

I particularly loved the visual of Michelle in the foundation garments for her huge dress. Scaffolding, it perfectly described the crinoline with the combination of satin bands and tulle panels. It would look like a white construction zone. The satin merry widow I thought Michelle should wear hooked up the back, but the unhooking of a front closure corset would be sexier in drawings.

I wasn't going to shy away from the gratuitous sex scenes for this, and I knew of at least one panel for their honeymoon story arc would have Michelle completely exposed. With a slight arch in her back, she would pose with her arms raised, enough to emphasize her breasts. Johnny would growl low in his throat before sucking a taut brown nipple into his mouth, and Michelle would purr "husband," with satisfaction, threading her fingers through his hair.

I shook my hand, trying to get the cramp out. I flipped back through the pages. That felt good. I got the images out of my head and onto paper. I was concerned that I wouldn't convey Johnny's level of frustration about the buttons down Michelle's back. I made sure to note 'really frustrated' next to that sketch.

I nodded to myself, this worked. It didn't suck. Well, at least, I thought it didn't. I needed to take a break and massage some life into my hand before I tackled the actual sex scene. This had to be an emotional scene, not just sexy. They were husband and wife, this was the consummating deed, and it sealed the deal. It had to be emotional and really hot.

The new and improved Michelle character may have grown up a good Catholic girl, but she didn't get where she was by not experiencing life. That was good—I didn't want to deal with the whole virgin thing. The original character, she was too sweet to have not been one.

I got up and stretched. It felt like I had been hunched over that notebook for minutes and not hours, while it had actually been quite a few hours. When I tried to move, my body told me it had been in that position for days. I padded over to my bathroom, and then headed downstairs to find a snack. I expected Mike to be up watching TV. Everything downstairs was dark. Mike must have locked up early and headed to bed. Well, I had thought it was early until I saw the clock on the microwave. It was well after midnight.

I shook my head, and changed my plans regarding the snack. Even with a set work schedule, I was up way too late again. This was a bad habit forming that I did not want. I really couldn't stay up late and expect to be able to function properly in the morning.

19

When the Peter Keith biopic came out, I watched it with Mike. Of course, it was released straight to cable. We both agreed that Liam James was a hottie, and had the potential to have a great career. I laughed when appropriate, and teared-up when appropriate. Clearly, John Lambert was not a fan of Michelle Cruz-Keith. At first, she was a sympathetic character. I even cheered for their relationship to make it. But, she was obviously painted as a bad guy when it came to enabling Peter's access to the drugs and pushing him to continue working when he really needed to take time off to recover and get some physical therapy.

Even though I had given up on the original story we had been working on for something different after Peter disappeared, I made mental notes of things that were too similar, and things I needed to change because they were exactly the same. Occurrences that would be obvious to anyone involved in Peter's life, that I should have no clue about being a complete stranger to him, needed changing.

After the movie was over, I excused myself. I went and took a shower. Not that I needed one, but I figured that would be the best way to drown the sounds of my sobs—watching his story hurt on a cellular level. I thought I had successfully gotten over him. I had not. I sat curled up on the shower floor until the water ran cold. I had known him. I really had, even if it had only been for a brief moment of time. He had been my lover and my friend—and he was gone. It was like he had died all over again.

I became angry and bitter after Peter disappeared without even saying goodbye. I've been ditched by friends before. It felt entirely too much like middle school—I'll be your friend until I find someone else who I think is cooler and might actually get me invited to better parties.

Like Peter's cheesy movies, his biography hit heavy rotation. The second time I watched it, I was alone, so I sat there and bawled the entire time. The third time, I almost broke the TV throwing the remote at it. The next time I saw that it was on, I grabbed a notebook and took notes. I had put entirely too much time into writing that story with and without his help. Peter be damned, I was going to keep working on it, and there were things that definitely needed changing, even with the help of Michelle Muse.

I was almost asleep, or maybe I was asleep, when I noticed Peter. I tried to roll over and ignore him. It had been a month since the initial broadcast of his biography.

I hurt and felt hollow, and tonight Peter chose to come back and sit at the foot of my bed like he had when all of this started so long ago. I must have been asleep, I could see him. He looked rough, haggard. I had no sympathy. Crying for a month straight did horrible things to one's complexion.

He had ruined mine, so he looked a little worse for wear. Welcome to the club.

I didn't say anything. I was angry. I felt like railing against him, he infuriated me so much. He had hurt me so completely. I wanted to curl into a ball to get away from him, not let him near so he couldn't hurt me anymore.

"I'm sorry, Gil," he began. He ran a hand through his hair and looked over at me. His eyes were that big soft brown. I normally would have melted if he had looked at me like that before. This time, I stared back at him. "I got so carried away by the movie. I think it's what I really needed."

"I figured." I tried to be as cold as possible.

"I'm not sure what's going to happen now, but..." he hesitated.

"You won't be coming here anymore," I finished for him.

"No, I still want to come see you, it's just, I won't be able to work on the book with you anymore. The movie was what I was looking for. Everything feels different. I feel different. I was such an idiot, I really had no clue how much I was being missed."

I huffed, blowing hard through my nose. "I told you about how much your fans missed you and you pouted about being unappreciated. You're still an idiot. You have no intensions of helping me work on the idea of mine you said you'd help me with. You never did." I raised my voice in a high mocking whine, "help me write the love story I deserve and I'll help you with that comic book you want to do." I dropped my voice back to normal. "Fuck you, Peter Keith. You used me. You manipulated me to help you, you interfered with my relationship, seduced me, made me fall in love with you, then when you were done with me, you left and ignored me."

"I'm here, aren't I?" His voice raised in anger. "I watched

over you when you were sick, and I came back when I realized how long it's been. Time works differently for me, Gil, I didn't realize I had be gone so long."

"I don't care. I clearly don't mean as much to you as I had thought." I tried not to raise my voice, but it dripped with poison. "Before, you had time to be with me every day. Now, I don't even deserve a quick check in for a month. It started with days, then weeks, now months. You didn't even bother to say goodbye, Peter. I had no idea what happened to you. And I have no way to contact you. For all I knew, you were no longer a ghost, you were gone-gone. It was like you died on me."

"Don't be like that, Gil."

"Like what? A hurt, jilted lover? That's what I am, aren't I?"

"No, that's not what you are. I didn't mean to hurt you. I was distracted by everything."

I didn't want to listen to him. He would sweet talk me back into whatever he wanted. He had that power over me. I was still in love with him, and it was working against me. It made it so he could hurt me. I didn't want to hurt anymore.

"Go away, Peter." Laying down, I wrapped the pillow around my head.

"I'll be back, Gillian."

"No, you won't," I said to the air. Peter was gone.

I didn't need Peter. I had a schedule and deadlines, and the Michelle Muse. And she started nagging me about needing a proper kitchen and that they were going to have to remodel the one in their house. She kept me distracted from having to deal with my emotions over this whole Peter being gone thing, so she got what she wanted.

Without much focus, I gave into the Michelle kitchen urge. I wrote notes and sketched consistently for hours. I had a complete story arc that helped to define Michelle's role in Johnny's life. Michelle Cole baked when she needed to think through a problem. Johnny might have to fight the bad guys, but Michelle baked her way to a conclusion, and she wanted a complete kitchen overhaul.

They lived in a nice house, but it was dated, built in the nineteen-sixties. The kitchen had seen a pretty big renovation in the nineteen-eighties but it didn't suit her needs. Michelle liked to bake, her husband was an up and coming action star and shape-shifting, secret vigilante. She deserved a renovated kitchen.

We didn't change the shape of the kitchen or even the general layout, but we did knock out a wall to create a pass through/counter island. Updating the range ate up some of the existing counter space. I did a little internet search and found the best one for her sense of style and her culinary wants. I selected a Bertazzoni gas range. That thing had six burners, a built in griddle, and double ovens. What appealed to me most was that it wasn't stainless, it came in red enamel with stainless steel accents.

Michelle may have wanted a new kitchen, but I was the designer. And I wanted to draw that range. The second I saw it, I knew it was on my personal wish list. All other appliances were updated, counter tops and cabinets replaced. I even added a touch-less faucet

At first, I thought they really needed to buy a new house, but the Michelle Muse convinced me they were not financially ready for that. Yes, Johnny was poised for a major career break-through, but he wasn't there, yet. Besides, this home was far enough out of the city she could take care of big cats at home, if needed.

It felt odd having a conversation through a storyline. I worked it all out on my own, but it truly felt as if I had someone to bounce ideas off of. But not like I was talking to a real person. Maybe there was some energy force that was the Michelle Muse because this didn't exactly feel like it was happening all on my own.

20

_____

Weeks passed. It could have been months for all I cared. Peter was gone, something I didn't want to admit. Half the time, I made myself too busy to worry about anything, the other half, I pined for him. I missed him and I couldn't tell anyone. Hell, I barely admitted it to myself. I channeled all my energy into my work, and my project.

"How do you feel about spending some quality time with me and a car?"

Trina chuckled, "What did you have in mind?"

"There's a medical illustrator in Oakland selling off her entire book collection. It's full of some sweet anatomy books and other resources. I've agreed to buy it all, but I need to go pick it up. I was thinking that we could do a little day trip there this week."

I could hear her humming over the phone, it was a positive indication.

"And I'll buy pizza at that fabulous Chicago style place," I bribed.

"Why don't you have them shipped?" she asked.

"I'm already forking over a few hundred bucks for at

least a thousand dollars' worth of books, I can't really afford to spend another hundred plus on shipping, especially when she's only a few hours away. Please, Trina," I pleaded, "This is a major score. I'll pay for gas. I need some good in my life right now."

"Be prepared to have to listen to the same movie all the way up and all the way back," she threatened. Sophie would be entertained on the drive by the in-car DVD system. We adults would be tortured by it.

"I can handle that!"

We agreed that Thursday would be the best day to get the books. I made arrangements with Adam that I wouldn't be in the office that day. He knew about my book score. I actually had tried to get him to get the department to purchase the collection. It was a very good collection, and worth every penny. When he said it wasn't going to happen, I decided to make them my personal collection. He gave me the time off because he knew I would bring the books in and use them at work anyway.

I emailed the lady in Oakland, and everything was set for Thursday.

"*Beep, beep.*" Trina texted me from her van. Sophie was ensconced; it made no sense to disturb her to come get me at the door. I slid into the passenger seat. I cast a quick glance at Sophie, already enthralled by her movie.

"Five bucks she's passed out before we make it to the freeway," I said.

"You're on, I say within the first five minutes after we're on the freeway," Trina countered.

"Now that there is money on it, she won't fall asleep for at least thirty minutes," I joked. We both lost. Sophie held out on us. She didn't fall asleep for almost an hour.

"How are you holding up?" Trina cut to the chase

regarding my lack of relationship. I missed Peter much more than I ever missed David. It was hard, and I felt stupid about it. I said as much.

"Honey, you fell in love with him, didn't you?" she asked.

"Of course I did, how could I not?" I confessed. "He was funny and charming, and hot as hell." I swiveled to make sure Sophie was out. "And he was the best lover. I couldn't have even imagined anything that, that..." I sighed. There were no words to describe what it felt like to have been touched by him—even if it had only been on a subconscious level.

"How long has it been since you last saw him?"

"He's been gone months and months, since just after that biographical movie on him aired. I think he got what he needed from that. Ya know, he had been going off for weeks at a time. I figured he realized I wasn't the cool kid anymore, found someone else to hang out with. Someone who could give him what he needed."

"What was that?" Trina's eyes darted to me quickly before returning to the road.

"I wish I knew," I sighed. I gave him everything I could think of. I helped him come up with a fictional recounting of his life in a way that would please him, I gave him love in a way I had never anticipated being able to do. I gave him validation. I started tearing up. Damn it.

I missed him and deep down, I felt guilty, like I had run him off with all our stupid little arguments. Getting pissed at him for wandering off for days, then weeks at a time. For not having trusted and believed in him when he had been so real. I was so selfish. I had liked having him around, and now he wasn't.

"Did you hear they are making a *Trouble Trouble* movie?" She broke the building silence. I had retreated into my thoughts. Again, being selfish, leaving Trina hanging. "I guess it's going to be called *Trouble Trouble Too*."

"I saw that. I understand they are having the actor who played Peter in the movie of his life play his role in it," I added.

"At least he'll look right for the part," she laughed. "Poor guy's career is going to be based on playing another actor. So, how's the book?" she asked.

"I tried to keep working on it, but it didn't work anymore without him. I've ditched the whole writing thing, and I've completely changed it up. I'm still going to make the book, now the story is all mine. I'm illustrating it, making it a graphic novel." Actually the graphic novel was so much easier for me to produce.

I'm a visual thinker. It had started getting hard to take all the pictures in my head that Peter had given me and turn them into words. I would always miss some key sensory description. With illustrations, the only sensory keys I was missing were smell and touch, and I could add those in with words. Now, I could show the world how strong and glorious Johnny Urban really was. I could show the pictures in my head directly. He still looked like Peter, but bigger, taller, more powerful, longer hair, and blue eyes.

"A graphic novel? Oh, Gil, that's going to be awesome," Trina cooed.

"It is." I was sure of it. "I'm still using big parts of the storyline Peter helped me to develop, but I'm putting my own twist on it."

"How so?" she prompted.

"I always thought Johnny Urban, the Peter character, needed to be something preternatural. Peter hated that idea. Hated it. I had tried vampires, wolves, fairies, all of that. He wouldn't have any of it. But I couldn't help but think—this guy is a shape shifter, and with his tawny and gold coloring, it had to be a tiger. So now, he's a were-tiger. I'm almost done with the first book."

"First book?" Trina guided the car through traffic as one freeway merged into another.

"Yeah. With graphic novels, they get fat pretty fast because of all the illustrations. I've divided it into three major plotlines. And I'm not ending it officially. I'm going to leave it open ended so if I want to build a serial, I can. I even have a title now." I was excited. It was the first time I had really talked to Trina about this.

I know when I had started writing with Peter it was all I could do not to shove the words down her throat, but this project, I played closer to the chest. I think I was more guarded because it was me on my own, I didn't have a creative partner I could blame. Also, and I'm not sure I would admit this to anyone, it was my way of mourning Peter finally.

"What's it going to be called?"

"*Tails from the Urban Jungle.* Cause his name is Johnny Urban. And tails is spelled T-A-I-L-S because he's a tiger."

"Do I get to see it when it's done?"

"Absolutely! Actually, I was hoping you'd be willing to proofread it for me?" I was a little concerned asking, it felt like I had been so detached recently, and now I was full of favors.

"I'd love to, Gil. The story you had me read was exciting, I bet with your amazing illustration skills it will be fantastic!"

"Oh, I hope so. It's kind of scary doing this on my own. But I'm gonna do it." I think I said it out loud more for me than for Trina. "Holly from work helped me come up with a production schedule. It's really going to happen."

"It's helping you get over him, isn't it?" Trina was full of accurate insights.

"Uh huh," I nodded. "It's still hard. I got this amazing sense of calm about him a while ago. I'm pretty sure he's moved on to whatever was next for him." I wasn't going to admit I tried to make him show up in my imagination and it never worked. I could get a tall blond guy who looked like Peter to walk into a room, but it was different. It was my imagination.

I dreamed of him a few times, but they were dreams, not him communicating with me via dreams. Once, I even had a lovely erotic dream about him, but it paled in comparison to the real thing. Now that he was gone, I could really tell the difference. He hadn't been my imagination. My imagination wasn't that good.

I watched the golden sun dried hills pass as we made our way north into more and more traffic.

"Hey, we are almost there, got those directions?"

I did. We were able to navigate our way into a north Oakland neighborhood, more Berkeley than Oakland.

It turns out the lady was retiring and moving to Hawaii. She was selling off years' worth of supplies as well as the books I had found online. I ended up spending way more money than the books had cost. I left with some really nice, high quality traditional illustration and painting supplies, including a top notch set of oil pastels, papers, and lots of frisket for making airbrush masks. I even bought her old airbrush, now I had a backup one. I felt like I had arrived as an illustrator—I owned more than one airbrush! She let us use her bathroom, which was much needed after our nonstop drive.

After loading the van with all my new found treasures, we were pleased to find out we were only a few blocks from the pizza place. This was the most amazing pizza I had ever had. I can't remember how I ever found it the first time, probably some art workshop. It was Chicago style, meaning it was a double decker, actual, pizza pie. The bottom layer was a deep dish cheese filled dream of pizza goodness, topped with another layer of chunky pizza sauce and more cheese, and pesto. We made obscene noises of pleasure as we sat and ate our lunch. Even Sophie enjoyed her share of the pizza, and it didn't include ketchup.

In true Trina planning ahead fashion, she brought a large thermal bag. It easily fit in five to-go pizza boxes. We filled it with six. We each purchased an extra three pizzas to transport home and freeze. This pizza was that good.

Sated with pizza ambrosia, Trina guided the mini-van back to the freeway and south toward home. I was glad the van rolled with ease. I was stuffed, overfull to the point of being uncomfortable. I couldn't move. I had enjoyed every single bite getting to that point. No regrets.

"That's it," I declared. "I'm ruined for pizza for the rest of my life. I need to move here for the food. I've got no boyfriend to keep me back, I've found true love and it's topped with pesto."

"Um, what about work? What about me? I'd miss you." Trina over dramatized her 'me.'

"Naw, you'd come visit me every week for your pizza allotment."

Trina giggled. "True. But, you'd still need to find a new job, and I thought you liked the one you have."

"Ah, reality interfering with my fantasy life," I complained.

"I thought you already did that when you broke up with David and started seeing Peter." She cleared her throat when she said 'seeing.' She meant having amazing fantasy sex with him, but she couldn't exactly say that with little parrot ears awake behind us.

I snorted. It was true. I had ditched the cheating flesh and blood man for the dead one. "That was so messed up," I moaned. "I mean, David really had been cheating on me, and with that freelancer no less." I laughed. "When I gave her a project I was worried she was trying to figure out how to take my job. In reality, she was sussing me up because she was stealing my man." I shook my head. "I was such a dope about it too. I kept looking for excuses to explain things. I never actually suspected anything. Granted, I thought he had gone a little loopy when he started becoming all image conscious and bought that Lexus. I should have known something was up when he stopped playing with the Doctor Who connection."

"He really did look like that actor," Trina agreed.

"I know, right?"

We were almost home when I remembered something.

"I almost forgot to tell you. Holly is making me join a singles club with her."

"A what?" Trina asked, her eyebrows knitting together as she glanced at me.

"A singles club. It's some kind of organized dating group. Sometimes, it's actual organized date activities like speed dating, and sometimes, it's a social meeting or activity," I explained.

"You're gonna start dating again? That's wonderful, Gil. I was afraid you were going to hold up and hide away from men forever."

"I've already done that. Besides, I'm really going to keep Holly company while she actively dates. If something happens, so be it. I'm not holding my breath or anything.

Plus, have you seen the pitiful excuses called men on online dating sites? I can't do that right now."

Mike was home by the time we got back. Instead of volunteering to help unload the car, he distracted Sophie with tickles in the living room while Trina and I unloaded my haul of goodies into the condo. We absolutely covered the table and part of the kitchen counter. That was fine, it was inside—I could relocate it later.

I hugged Trina for all her help before she and Sophie left.

~

Life continued. I went to work; I had lunch with my friends. With a little help, I self-published a graphic novel, and then a second one. I was invited to sit on an author panel at a local comic convention. I met people who read my book. People I didn't know.

I published a third installment of *Tails from the Urban Jungle*, and suddenly, I had fans. I was invited to another local comic convention. There were people dressed up like my characters. There was actual Johnny Urban and Michelle Cole cos-play. I cried.

There was a demand for more books. I was prepared for none of it. And I couldn't share it with Peter. I hoped wherever he was, he saw the results of what he started. I wanted to yell out into the night and hoped he heard, "*Hey Peter, are you happy now? Is this what you were looking for? Look what I did for you, because of you. Are you even a little bit pleased? Are you proud of me?*"

I wanted him to be proud of me. I wanted him to see what I had accomplished. He may have only gotten the ball rolling, and it felt like he abandoned me in the middle of it all, but none of this could have happened without him. I wanted him to see it. I wanted him to know how incredibly thankful I was for all of it, his friendship, his love, his inspiration.

At the end of every book, tucked away so people didn't question me, I placed a small "for Peter," in one of the image panels. So far, no one had asked me about it.

21

The past few months of going out with Holly's singles club hadn't been a total waste of time either. Some of the activities were group outings, and if I hit it off with someone, great, if not, I still got to do something interesting. If I wasn't going out with her, I would have spent all of my free time nose deep in creating the Johnny Urban graphic novels. We went to the party restaurants with video games, we went cosmic bowling, we took painting classes, and we had old fashioned picnics in parks.

My favorites so far were the horseback riding and the cooking classes. I hadn't been on a horse in ages, like since I was eight or nine at summer camp. I had developed a little fantasy about falling in love with the trail guide, a real cowboy. He would help me up on my mount, and I would slip back into his arms. We would gaze deeply into each other's eyes and just know. He would lead my horse up front, next to his. I'm not sure how, but we would slip away from the group, and I would end up on his horse with him. It was all so romantic, until we actually met the trail guide.

I'm not even certain he was human. He looked more like an animated piece of jerky, smelled like old stale cigars and beer, and I think he may have had three teeth. I might be being generous. The horseback riding fantasy was a bust, but the trail ride had been a lot of fun, even if my backside and inner thighs hated me by the end of the day.

The cooking classes were my favorite. I know a few guys became interested after watching me have so much fun while learning to cook. I went to the classes for the cooking, not the people. Sorry, but I was not interested in auditioning to be their future glorified house keeper and live-in chef.

I never thought I would enjoy cooking, but I learned that it didn't have to be difficult in order to taste good. Cooking at home was healthier and so much cheaper than eating out all the time. Mike certainly enjoyed my cooking, and we started a deal where he paid for groceries if I cooked.

Holly and I went to every speed dating meeting they hosted. These were always an entertaining hour, followed by a more entertaining evening of nachos, margaritas, and comparing horror stories. For me, a date had to accomplish a few things to not be a complete waste of time—it had to introduce me to someone I would like to see a second time, or it had to be a good source for future mocking. If I couldn't walk away with at least one 'what the hell' moment to share with everyone I knew, then the date was a total waste of time.

After the break up with David, and getting ditched by Peter, I really wasn't interested in second dates with anyone. I honestly didn't really trust anyone enough anymore. I wasn't completely over either man, and probably wouldn't be for a while. After all, I did love each, and they each broke my heart in their own way. I now needed to learn to be a whole person without a partner. If one landed in my lap, I wouldn't say no. But I didn't actively seek out a replacement boyfriend. Months without one had proven I could be me alone, and I was okay.

I was interested in collecting as much crazy bad date fodder as I possibly could. The Johnny Urban graphic novels were actually selling, and had developed a bit of a cult following. I was in the middle of developing a *Perils of Dating While Single* series, something that could be sexy and funny. I started leaving a notebook in the car, so that as soon as each date was over, I could take notes on some of the more awkward moments, or just plain crazy things that happened.

I toyed with the idea of opening an account with a few online dating sites, but I was getting plenty of material from the singles club, and following along as Holly's second on double dates with her. Maybe if I ran out of material, but for now, I didn't need that particular hassle.

Tonight, we were in store for another speed dating meeting. We arrived about fifteen minutes early, as usual. Holly liked to check out the crowd before we began. I liked to be surprised. I had a bad habit of setting myself up for disappointment. Guys who appeared as if they would be nice tended to have the opposite personality. I found that if I removed any chance for me to prejudge a person, I was more open during the five minute discussion, and less disappointed from any expectations. I tried to be a decent human. It never lasted long, especially since as soon as the speed dates were over, I was the first one to start making fun of the whole event.

Everyone scattered throughout the room. Chairs and tables had been set up in a big circle. Some people sat, some milled about waiting for it to begin. Holly and I huddled close together trying to decide if we wanted Mexican or the sports bar afterwards. I was leaning toward the bar. The bartender was really hot, and I felt like wings were the perfect food tonight.

"Ah-hem." The club organizer stood in the front of the circle of tables. He had a hat that he held in front of him. "Okay, I recognize a few of you." He nodded toward Holly and me. "And some of you are new. So, let me explain how this works. We have twelve ladies and eleven gentlemen tonight, so we finish after all the ladies have a five minute date with all the gentlemen. We'll be done in an hour. I need a lady to draw from the hat to see which group is on the inside."

A woman with black hair, in a red strapless dress with matching red lipstick, pulled a piece of paper from the hat. I felt incredibly underdressed having come straight from work. She handed the organizer the slip of paper. "Alright, ladies you will be on the outside ring, which means you move and the men will have the inner ring, and they stay in place. I'm going to ask you now to stand behind a chair. Remember ladies, on the outer ring, please. Since we have more ladies tonight there will be an empty space. You get a five minute date with air."

There was shuffling around as everyone found a chair to stand behind. I smiled at the guy across from me. He looked nice enough—Sandy hair, Dockers, and a light blue button-down shirt. I reminded myself to not assume personality based on appearance.

"When the alarm sounds you can begin. Ladies, please move to your left on the next alarm."

He sounded a buzzer, and we sat.

I extended my hand, as did my date.

"Gillian, how are you today?"

"Jim, and I'm doing great. Wanna get out of here and get laid when this is over. I live about five minutes away."

And score one for Gillian's bad judgment. I had a 'let's get laid' right out of the starting gate. I zoned out and smiled and nodded, and thought about how extra hot sauce on wings would be good tonight. I contemplated the merits of blue cheese versus ranch for dipping sauce until the buzzer sounded.

I left let's-get-laid-Jim and moved to my left. The woman next to me shifted right, and we had a minor crash. Apologies and giggles over the confusion, it happens every time, and it would happen at least one more time tonight before everyone shifted with precision.

My next date was Tad. Tad was in car sales. Tad was really interested in what I drove and thought he could get me into a newer Toyota for a reasonable price. He slipped me his business card. There was always at least one sales guy, usually someone with a multi-level marketing brand. I think they were so used to selling things, they forgot that now was the time to sell themselves and not their products.

After Tad, I landed another lets have sex guy. I didn't even bother to remember his name. What I did remember was the expression on my neighbor's face when she turned to me as we were switching. Her eyes were crazy and her brows drawn together. Clearly, she signaled that this was not a high quality five minutes I was stepping up to.

My fourth date was a complete surprise.

"David?" I had not expected him to be at a dating event. I figured he was still with Jenny. I said as much.

"We aren't together anymore."

I nodded. I didn't want to know, but at the same time, I

did want to know why not. He had blown a good thing with me for her.

"Why?" My curiosity got the better of me.

"It's really none of your business." He huffed through his nose.

I raised my hands in surrender. "I'm not going to say anything, I'm not here to argue or discuss what ifs."

Hell, I didn't really even want to talk to him anymore. I folded my arms and turned my focus toward the floor. David did the same. We would never be friends again. For whatever reason, he was single again, and I hoped it had been as ego crushing as finding out he had been cheating on me.

My time with David was an excruciating long five minutes.

The next guy had the unfortunate position of being after David. I barely remember anything about him except he had cats. I spend most of my time fuming about David. Tattoo boy was next. From what I could see, he was covered from his knuckles to his neck. I didn't mind tattoos, but it was the only memorable thing about him.

When the buzzer sounded, I noticed the next guy was big. Like, football player big. He had thick shoulders about a mile wide. When I stepped in front of him, a huge smile crossed his handsome face, exposing incredibly white teeth. He had naturally tan skin, his brown hair was long to his shoulders and in dreads. His features made me think he was part Pacific Islander, Samoan or Hawaiian. He had a wide mouth, and a straight nose that was slightly on the wide side. His jaw was incredibly square. Then I looked at his eyes, and felt all the blood leave my body. The same brow line, the same color and shape, they were Peter's eyes.

I felt tears sting my own, and I gasped out his name. "Peter." My hand flew to my mouth as I realized what I had done. I was so embarrassed. I had just called this incredibly good looking guy who in no way resembled Peter Keith, except for the eyes, Peter.

"Hi, Gilligan." He smiled then reached forward and bopped me on the nose. "I've been looking for you."

I know my jaw dropped open. I was speechless. Tears escaped my eyes.

"My name is Brand." He nodded. "But, um. I remember you. I remember everything from my life as Peter."

I stared at him. "Brand." I could barely whisper. But it was Peter with a different face and body. "How?"

He looked at the watch on his wrist. His forearms rippled with muscle, bands of patterned tattoos circled his arm. Peter, I mean Brand, was huge, all muscle. He had to be a body builder.

"We're almost out of time. Meet me out front when this is over?"

The buzzer sounded while I nodded.

I reluctantly shifted to the next guy. I kept looking back at Peter. *Brand.* I had to think of him as Brand. It was him. Every cell in my body recognized him—my brain was having a hard time catching up.

My date repeated something urgently.

"I'm sorry, what?" I had not been paying attention.

"Are you okay? You're crying. Did that jerk say something to you to upset you? Should I report him?" I sat across from a nice guy, he seemed genuinely concerned.

"No, no, I'm fine. Turns out we both have a mutual friend who died." I waved my hand trying to dry up my tears. "Unexpected memories, nothing more."

I glanced back at Brand when it was time to move again. I ended up at the empty table. That was fine. It gave me an opportunity to stare at a small section of his shoulder, all that I could see from this angle. I didn't know how I was going to be able to finish this. I started counting the men. I had three more five minute dates after this. Fifteen minutes before I'd be able to talk to Brand again.

The buzzer sounded, and I shifted again. I introduced myself, my date did the same, his name was David. I began babbling.

"I'm sure you've already heard this tonight, but you're the second David I've talked to. I used to date the other one. Until then, he was the only David I can remember having met. After we started dating, I started to meet a lot of guys named David. I'm guessing it's just I was all of a sudden aware of the name. Do you meet a lot of people with the same name? I've never met anyone with my name before. It's a family name so it's not exactly on any baby name lists. As a kid, I could never find those souvenirs with my name on it. They always had David, so I bet you got lots of those as a kid since you could find your name."

From the expression on David number two's face, I must have prattled on nonstop the entire time. The next five minutes were passed in boring tedium as I was the one stuck pretending to listen as the guy across from me babbled on. I guess it was instant karmic payback. He either talked about networked video games or work. I wasn't really certain, but I did hear the word server several times. Maybe he wasn't talking about computers at all but waitresses and waiters. I didn't pay attention. Peter, Brand, was right over there, and I had to play nice before I could talk to him again.

One last date. These five minutes were longer than the time I spent with my ex, David. I admitted to the guy across from me that I either talked too much or didn't pay enough attention. He barely spoke at all. I ended up spending the last few minutes staring at the floor and chewing my thumbnail in awkward silence waiting for the buzzer. As soon as it sounded, I made for the door. I didn't know what I was going to do once I was on the other side of it. I wanted to pound on Peter for abandoning me, because that's what it still felt like. I also wanted to jump into his arms and hold him and kiss him. I still loved him.

I beat Brand outside by eight pacing steps. He walked out the door and stood there. I stared at him. He was bigger now. Brand was not only wide through the shoulders, he was much taller than Peter had been. I didn't say anything. Everything I wanted to say, everything I thought about in the past fifteen minutes, it was all gone. He was Peter—I could feel it in my bones. Everything about him, except his outward appearance, was Peter.

He took a small step toward me. "Gil." His voice was soft, and I lost it. I threw myself into his arms sobbing. It felt familiar and foreign all at once.

"You left me," I managed to say between gulping for air.

"I didn't mean to. This happened, and it took so much longer than I thought it would."

I pushed back to look at him. I stepped away and he leaned against the wall. I hugged myself. He glanced up and down the hall, to see if it was clear.

"What happened?" I asked, my voice small, barely able to escape my throat.

"My name is Brandon Paulo, until six months ago I was a professional football player. One day I took a hit and flat lined on the practice field. They said I suffered a traumatic brain injury."

Holly rushed through the door. "There you are, Gil. I was looking for.... Oh hi... you're Brand, right?" She looked from him to me a few times. "Oh, you two are, okay." She turned to me, "I'll just be inside when you're ready to go."

She then mouthed 'bring him for drinks,' before she went back into the meeting room.

Brand nodded. "I always thought Holly was nice. Especially when she brought you soup when you were sick."

My eyes started leaking like crazy, not that I wasn't already on the verge of crying again. But he had confirmed something that the only people who knew where Holly, myself, and my ghost.

"Oh my God, Peter." I covered my mouth again. I was in shock.

"It's been a wild recovery. I don't know how I woke up in this body, and I don't really know what happened to Brandon. I'm not joking when I say I remember everything from being Peter. That includes you. Your hair's grown out a bit. I like it."

He kept his distance. But he looked like a big cat coiled and ready to pounce. "This body suffers from retrograde amnesia. More of Brandon's memories are coming back, and I can remember things once someone has reminded me about them. I'm still missing big chunks of Brand's past, my past." He paused, holding his hands out in supplication. "I have so much to make up to you, and Holly is in there waiting for you. Can I call you sometime, so we can talk?"

I nodded. I was perfectly willing to stay here in the hallway and listen to him for hours.

"I want to show you something." Brand began unbuttoning his shirt. I got glimpses of an incredibly well-defined chest and warm caramel skin. He unbuttoned about half the buttons, and then he pulled the shirt to expose the flesh of his left shoulder and pectoral. The combination of physique and what he showed me made all moisture leave my mouth.

Tattooed across his shoulder and covering a good portion of the left side of his chest was a tiger prowling through a stand of bamboo. The work was beautifully executed and had an Asian look to it. He clearly had had the tattoo for quite a while as some of the colors were faded. I tentatively reached forward to touch it. I paused as I realized what I was doing. I was about to reach out and caress this man's tattooed chest. Technically, he was still a stranger, even though he was Peter. I pulled my hand back and bit my thumbnail.

"I always thought a tiger suited you," I laughed. "I've got something to show you too."

I reached into my bag and pulled out a slightly bent copy of the first *Tails from the Urban Jungle*. I carried one with me most of the time to show off.

"I made Johnny Urban a were-tiger after you left." I flipped through the book, then opened it wide to the page I was looking for. Spread across two pages was a full color illustration of a blond man with exceptionally broad shoulders and a very similar tiger tattoo across half of his chest. I handed Brand the book.

He held it reverently. "You did it. This is awesome, Gilligan. Shit, I always knew you were really good." He smiled as he flipped through the book. He began reading the back cover, "Denver's story telling ranks her among the grandfathers of American twentieth century sci-fi adventure, William Powers Stapleton and Edgar Rice Burroughs. Johnny Urban is a modern hero that joins the ranks of Flash Gordon, Sebastian Hale, and Tarzan."

His mouth hung open a little when his gaze returned to my face.

"Keep it." I nodded, turning my focus to my phone. "Okay, what's your phone number?" I programmed his number in, then immediately called him. He programmed my number into his phone too. "You are going to call me tonight." It wasn't a question, we needed to continue this conversation, but he was right, I was keeping Holly waiting.

"A few more things you need to know, 'cause I know as soon as you and Holly get to your margaritas, you're going to look me up online. I don't want you finding this out from the internet okay. So like, I'm from a kind of family that's done stuff. My father was an Olympic runner and was on cereal boxes, and my sister is some kind of dancer in the movies."

I nodded. Okay, so he came with some celebrity credit. I would have to figure out how to deal with that later, right now, I had to deal with Peter, Brand, being here.

"There's more. I have a five year old son. His name is Devon. His mother and I aren't together. We were never married. She seems like a nice person, she lets me see him, and she showed me his baby pictures while I was in the hospital to help me remember. She's married now, so our relationship is only because of Devon. He's a pretty amazing kid. I didn't want you to find that out and start making up wild stories in your head like you do."

I bit my nail and nodded at him. He knew me. I pulled the door open and was stepping through.

"One more thing, Gillian, I'm still in love with you."

I felt the air leave my lungs. Peter had crappy timing. I stood inside the door. It swung shut behind me. Peter finally admitted to being in love with me. After all this time, he finally said the words. I pushed back through the door. He was walking down the hall.

I called after him, "If you don't call me tonight, I'll kill you all over again, Peter Keith!"

He smiled at me. It was broad and full of gleaming white teeth.

Brand called me two hours after I met him. He said he waited as long as he could, giving Holly and me time to have wings and beer. We were still at the bar when he called. I called him back as soon as I got home. I tried not to rush through my evening with Holly, but I wanted, no, I needed to talk to Brand. After a very long phone conversation, I knew he was Peter. All doubts were gone, not that I had any.

22

W e met the next day for a very long lunch date. When I arrived at the arranged restaurant, he had a bouquet of mixed flowers for me. I think he was the first man to bring me flowers. I sat and he talked. I could hardly believe he came back, but here he was, and he wanted me. He never meant to abandon me. I didn't know if I should trust him or not. But it was hard keeping him at a distance. I had missed him so much, and I still loved him equally as much.

He mentioned all the ways he let me down. I didn't have to tell him, he knew. He wanted to make it all up to me. He even brought up helping me develop the story concept of the psychic girl who saw messages in the hair on the tub wall. He said everything I desperately needed to hear. He couldn't get into my head any more, this proved to me he had been paying attention.

My plans were to slowly ease back into a relationship with him. I invited him over to meet Mike, and to hang out the next Sunday. I was going to have to figure out when he could meet Trina. She wasn't going to believe this. Then again, I might not tell her who he was. Of course I would, I was thinking crazy for a minute.

I had thought Brand was big but he was even bigger once he was inside, confined by walls and a ceiling. He seemed even taller and broader in an enclosed space. He moved through the condo as if he had been there before. I knew he had as Peter, but it was disconcerting to actually see him physically there, even if it was in a different body.

He helped me with my Sunday grocery shopping, and now sat on his usual stool as I did my food prep for the week.

"If you tell me what to do, I can help," he said leaning over the counter. He even tried to look down my shirt, like always.

I glared at him. The best part of that was that I could actually see him. My glare didn't last long before it turned into a grin.

"You seem awfully happy, Gilligan." He noticed.

"Why wouldn't I be? You're actually here." I was stupid-happy, and torturing myself. I wanted nothing more than to drag him upstairs and rip his clothes off. But, I had just met him, well this embodiment of him. I tried to be a responsible adult. I'd rip his clothes off later. I wasn't specific with myself how much later. "Okay, come here and start chopping."

I handed him the knife. I watched as he carefully and slowly sliced through the onion. It was like he had never cut vegetables before. I had to remind myself that his body had amnesia, and Peter had probably never cooked.

I began making my weekly batch of hummus. I was finally able to give him a taste of my cooking. The look of amazement on his face when he tried the hummus made me feel really good about my skills. I smiled like a fool when

Mike came in. Brand and I stood working side-by-side in the kitchen laughing. He kept smiling at me, and I at him.

Mike looked like he was going to start drooling as he checked Brand out. Brand hadn't noticed, but I saw Mike's gaze appreciatively rake up and down Brand's physique. Brand was physically very commanding at six-five with long dark dreads. His mixed heritage of Pacific Islander and Anglo, and African-American gave his skin a soft warm color. Even though he could no longer play football, he continued to lift weights. He had pecs that should be classified as weapons, they were so well-muscled. He was built like an inverted triangle, and his butt in jeans was a thing of beauty.

"Hey Mike, this is Brand. He's my..." I paused, I was about to call him boyfriend but I needed to run that by Brand first. I hoped he wanted to be my boyfriend for a very long time. "My new friend."

"Really, Gilligan? My new friend?" Brand turned to Mike extending his hand. Mike took it. "I'm her boyfriend, and future fiancé."

"You're certainly confident, and large," Mike managed. He was a bit taken aback. So was I. I think we were both staring at Brand with slack jaws.

Brand had a deep hearty laugh. Mike took over perching on the stool while Brand and I worked in the kitchen. They got along, and I sensed a budding bromance. I was still having a hard time believing I finally had Peter in a physical body. I smiled like an idiot all afternoon.

Mike left to meet friends for dinner. I think he made an excuse to leave for a few hours so we could be alone. Just as I thought I should drag Brand up to my room, he swept me up into his arms and carried me upstairs. I giggled with excited anticipation. I loved every second that he touched me. He could touch me, and I could touch him, and I was awake.

Brand certainly seemed to remember how to kiss. Then again, maybe it was the Peter memory that guided him. "I'm pretty sure I remember how to do this," he said after I made a smart-ass comment about it.

Brand's lips were warm and soft. Softer than Peter's had been. I needed to stop comparing then and now—same spirit, same love, different body. I had thought the Peter Keith body had been pretty wondrous. Smooth skin, ticklish hairs, firm muscles, amazing fingers and lips. But Brand Paulo's body was mind blowing, and I hadn't even seen all of it yet.

"I missed you," I moaned into his mouth as he kissed me more.

He reverently removed my clothes. His hands were amazingly large, and I felt remarkably delicate as he ran his hands across my collarbone and down my arms. His touch was gentle as he took me in through his fingertips. His expression said he was just as amazed at touching me, as I was by being touched by him.

I had to stand on my tip toes to reach around his neck and pull him down to me. I wanted his mouth against mine. He lifted me into his embrace, holding me close against his chest, without crushing me. He held me like I was made of fine bone china. His clothes felt rough against my sensitized skin. All of my nerve endings were alive with anticipation—and they were all exposed.

He placed me on my bed. I stood, towering over him. He smiled, laughing up at me as I had to bend over to keep kissing him. I straightened and he placed kisses between my breasts, before pulling me closer and claiming more of my body with his mouth. I loved the eroticism of being nude while he was dressed, but I was also eager to touch him skin on skin.

Brand had focus and his lips kept me distracted from remembering I needed to remove his clothes. He trailed kisses lower on my abdomen. His hands braced me, holding my legs and butt firmly in place. I tangled my fingers in his hair, letting the locks twist and twine with my fingers. I loved the look on his face as he kissed me, eyes closed against high cheek bones.

I'm glad he braced me so thoroughly, because my knees buckled when he lowered his mouth farther and began sucking on my sex. I grabbed his hair for support. I could hardly breathe. Brand knew exactly what he was doing. His tongue was more magical than I remembered. He definitely had to be able to breathe through his ears to accomplish what he was doing.

I cried out before remembering to stifle the sounds I wanted to make. Even though Mike wasn't home, our walls were thin enough I had to watch my noises for the neighbors on the other side. When Brand pulled away from me, he grinned large and wide.

I wanted more—more of him touching me, more of his tongue, more of his skin, more of his love. Brand lowered me to the bed, and then began undressing. He pulled his T-shirt off over his head. My mouth went dry. His abs were a washboard of defined muscle, he had almost no chest hair, but a thin line of dark hairs led from his bellybutton and disappeared into his waistband.

He watched me as I assessed his physique. I couldn't have drawn a more splendid specimen. He tossed his shirt to the side, and then pulled on his belt. My God, the bulge in the front of his jeans was impressive. He reached down and lifted his foot to pull off his shoes, one leg at a time. It wasn't exactly a strip tease, but it was a tease all the same. I couldn't lay there and watch anymore. I rose up on my knees and began tracing the tattoos on his chest and shoulder. The tiger tattoo covered half of his chest—it integrated with geometric tribal markings that covered his shoulder and down his arm past his elbow.

I traced his tiger tattoo delicately with my fingers, tickling him. I loved his giggle, and his smile. He had muscles on top of muscles, and he giggled. His body was amazing. His skin was smooth and his muscles were tight and hard, like velvet covered rocks. I know I gaped when he was finally completely nude in front of me. I thought he had been slightly larger than proportional before, but now—whoa. Brand was exceptionally proportional. My first thought was I would need a hinged jaw to accommodate all of it when I turned him into my personal lollipop. My second thought was I was going to be ruined for any man after this. I smiled at that thought. I wouldn't need any other man after Brand. If I had anything to say in the matter, there wouldn't be any one after him, I would be perfectly happy with this man for the rest of my life.

Everything felt a million times better while conscious than it ever had on the dream plane. I needed more hands to touch him. I couldn't touch enough of him at once, and I needed to touch all of him. I tasted as much of him as I could. His skin was salty, and he smelled of exotic spices. Brand hissed when I laved one brown nipple.

I licked the tiger, almost expecting it to taste different to my tongue. I trailed my tongue over his shoulder following the ink work to his back. I kissed across and down his back. I don't know if I ever kissed down anyone's back before, but it didn't matter. I wanted to kiss all of him, claim him with my lips. I scraped my teeth across his ass, it was insanely well-muscled and firm.

"No biting," Brand protested as he rolled over and grabbed me. My trail of kisses across his body interrupted. My lips didn't protest at all, they were distracted by his lips again. I was back underneath him. He held himself up with straightened arms. Our mouths were busy twining tongues, my hands caressed his muscled arms. I dug my fingers into his triceps. He had the arms of a superhero. His knee moved between my legs, they wrapped around his hips in invitation.

I wanted to cry with joy when he finally entered me. Brand thrust and I lost my breath as I accommodated all of him. He felt familiar, yet better. I pushed dreads away from his face as he looked down at me. I loved his long dark hair. I loved his expression of fierce concentration as he made love to me. And with the emotion exuding from all of my pores, this wasn't sex, this was physical love at its finest.

His skill and movement inspired noises of elation. The more he thrust, the more sound I made. I finally had to shove a pillow over my face to muffle the screams of joy. When I reached my personal rapture, Brand continued to work me until it almost felt like torture. For him, reaching orgasm was just the beginning, muscle function in my lower body was controlled by his thrusts.

I didn't have star bursts and fireworks when I came. I had the big bang, the forming of the universe, birth of stars and solar systems. I saw planets collide to form other planets, and stars exploding in super nova bursts. If Brand continued to do what he was doing to me, I would know the secrets to creation and see the true face of God.

Brand's growl of satisfied completion brought me back to earth. I did see the face of the gods, they all looked like

Brand Paulo. He rolled over onto his back, pulling me across his chest. I pushed up on my elbows, so I could focus on his beautiful face, those big brown eyes on me.

"I love you, Gillian," his voice was full of emotion. His fingers toyed with the hair around my face.

"I can't tell if I'm talking to Brand or Pete. They're his words, but it's your voice," I confessed

"They are both me," he said.

"So when I say I love you Peter, you won't get mad or be hurt that I call you by the wrong name?"

"No, we're one and the same." He chuckled, his hands stroking up and down my back.

"I'm in love with Peter Keith, I guess that means I'm also in love with Brandon Paulo," I said, studying his face.

"So, how soon before you marry me?"

I laughed, "Your boyfriend status didn't last long, did it? Fiancé now, huh?"

"I take that as a yes, that you will marry me." He smiled. "I messed up my life the first go round. I'm going to do it right this time. I need you to be complete. You helped me to realize what I need to be a better person. I need you to make me a better man."

"I guess then I'll say yes." It was hard to kiss him I smiled so hard.

23

---

about a year later

"No, I swear, she would be perfect. If she was ten or fifteen years younger."

I stared at my ankles, they were propped up on a pillow in front of me, and they were swollen. "She's practically in her fifties, she's supposed to be twenty-five. Yes, she's still gorgeous, but she's gonna look like his mother." Actually all of me felt swollen. Thirty-eight weeks and counting.

Brand hadn't kept his fiancé status much longer than he did his boyfriend status. He quickly advanced to husband, and now, impending father.

"We need an unknown, but I don't want someone who everyone is going to say is a young so-and-so."

Tails from the Urban Jungle had been picked up for a cable series. That meant it could be as hot and sexy, if not more so, than originally written. I was on the phone with my agent. She called to discuss some casting options. I knew who was in my dream cast. I was hoping they kept my characters at least close to their original descriptions. I kept fighting with the studio over who would be appropriate for Michelle.

They kept trying to white-wash her. Her ethnicity was key to her character, and they needed to stop trying to get blonde Swedish actresses to play her. I was glad I had insisted on having a say on the casting in the contract. I trusted them regarding acting skill, but I was very particular about the visual presentation—the two actresses from my dream list that would be perfect were too expensive and a touch too old.

My agent said she had called with a surprise. So far, discussing the casting problems regarding the Michelle Cole character did not qualify as a surprise. It had been an on-going issue for the past six weeks.

I was tired, and ready to not deal with this. I was really hoping all of this would have been settled before I was ready to not do anything but have a baby. I passed that point two days ago.

"You promised me some good news, this wasn't it was it?"

"No, Gil, that wasn't it. So, are you sitting down?" she asked.

"It's all I ever do these days."

This pregnancy had been going perfectly. I had morning sickness for a text-book perfect three months. I looked like I had swallowed a basketball. Nothing else 'got pregnant,' my face barely changed, nothing was swollen, my butt hadn't gotten bigger, honestly, and I hadn't even gained that much weight. I hovered around the ideal gain of twenty five pounds my doctor wanted for me.

I was still relatively active until my ankles decided it was time to swell. The rest of me swelled up soon after. As soon as that happened, I was put on restricted activity and lots of bed rest. My doctor announced that maternity leave started immediately. It had only been a few days but I already started to go stir crazy. I wasn't allowed to do anything. Anything.

Brand fussed over me. It was like his first pregnancy, he didn't remember when Devon's mother had been pregnant, and Peter had never been a father. He was actually quite cute and endearing. It helped that I did like him taking care of me. But, I still wanted to be able to do things for myself, instead of being stuck sitting on the couch all day long.

"They got him, Gil!" she announced proudly.

I sat up more.

"Really?" I started a wiggly dance of happiness while on my butt.

"He's signed, and he's hitting the gym to bulk up!"

"YES!"

Liam James was contracted to play Johnny Urban!

EPILOGUE

A little over five years later

"Hey Gil! You came." A low, bright cherry red, vintage Corvette with can-opener flames rumbled to a stop in front of Brand and I. Liam James beamed at us with a bright toothy grin from the driver's seat.

"Liam, dude, you invite us to a wrap party and leave just as we arrive," Brand pointed out.

Liam reached out of the car window, and the two men bumped knuckles.

I crossed my arms and tried to work my mom-look on Liam. It worked on the five year old at home, but apparently Liam was immune to my motherhood. I had tried it on him before, when we were filming the show to no avail. My kids were infants at that point. But I had refined that look in the past couple of years. However, it still didn't work on Liam.

"I'll be back in a few. I want to see what this baby can do on the open road."

"Really Liam? Really? I have toddlers at home, I don't get

to go to Hollywood parties anymore. Take the car out for a joy ride later. Don't make me go in there by myself," I may have whined as I flapped my hand in the direction of the sound stage with an obvious party going on.

"What am I chopped liver?" Brand asked with a chuckle as he bumped his shoulder against mine.

My husband was far from chopped liver, he was grade-A prime rib, beef cake with legs. But he was retired from the NFL, he wasn't Hollywood. At least, no one knew he had a past life that was all Hollywood all the time. Brand's sister Emi was an actress, but she wasn't around, and I hadn't been involved in anything Hollywood since shooting *Tails from the Urban Jungle* wrapped.

"Let the man have his fun," Brand said. "We can navigate a party just fine."

"Have his fun? He's been driving around in this"— I turned to Liam and placed my hand on the top of the rumbling car— "what, for the past nine weeks? You've had plenty of time to play with your new toy."

Liam shook his head. "Filming went fast, six weeks. And after today I have to say goodbye to this gorgeous lady."

He caressed the steering wheel. That's when I noticed it was on the wrong side of the car.

"They aren't letting me buy her. I wasn't allowed to really open her up and see what she can do. In all the driving scenes this baby was mounted on a rig, and the speed was wind machines and green screen." He revved the engine to emphasize his point. He was in a fierce machine designed to eat up the road and spit it back out. "I'll be right back, before they notice I borrowed the car."

Liam flashed another dazzling smile as the car shot down the street.

Honestly, I'd want to take the car out and drive fast too. There was something primal about speed, and being in control of it.

"Stop him!" A guy came running around the corner of the sound stage. He huffed and puffed as his legs carried him along the same direction that Liam had driven off in. He made it a couple dozen yards before he slowed and eventually stopped before bracing against his thighs and lowering his head.

Brand jogged up to the guy. "You good man?"

I wasn't nearly as quick, but the kids at home had me in slightly better shape than the guy staring off after the car, that was no longer in sight. His face was beat red, and he was sucking in air with deep heavy breaths. I had no idea how far he had run, maybe he was in better shape than me.

"Was that James?"

"Yeah," I said.

"Damn it. Where did he say he was going?" The guy stood and swept his ball cap off as he swiped sweat from his brow.

I shrugged.

"Said he wanted to see what she can do," Brand answered.

The guy threw the hat to the ground. "Fuck! Fuck, fuck, fuck. That idiot!" He stomped around in a circle. After he threw his hissy fit he leaned over and scooped up his hat before shaking it in the direction the car had driven off. "It's like he never listens. I swear. I have to go let Benny know."

He lifted his eyes to the sky, closed them, and took a deep breath. "Please don't let this be bad."

"What's the matter? He's just gone for a short drive," I pointed out.

The guy shook his head before opening his eyes and locking gazes with me. "That car is for show. It's nothing more than a prop." He shook his head again.

"Does Liam know that?" I asked.

"He was told that every time he asked to take it for a drive. But he refused to believe anyone."

Brand snorted. "That sounds like Liam to me."

"Well, I need to find Benny and let him know. Let's just hope the idiot doesn't get himself killed." he started to storm back toward the sound stage. I assumed he meant Benny Skye, the producer. I never met the man, I only knew him by name.

"What do you mean, get himself killed?" I called out after him. It took me a few steps to catch up, and I matched his rushed pace.

He held up his hand and started a finger by finger count out. "One, that car is not street legal. Two, it looks like it can go fast, it cannot. Three, it only has a right hand drive because of some tricky rigging with a chain drive. It's not capable of responding in a timely fashion."

Before he flipped out a fourth finger, he balled his hand into a fist. "It's fiber glass and duct tape. If he hits a pot hole that car shaped prop is in danger of crumbling. And if it crumbles while he's doing anything over twenty five, he's going to get hurt."

I stopped walking and turned to gaze back in the direction Liam had left in. The guy continued on his mission to alert Benny to the situation.

"Don't worry about him, Gil." Brand stepped up to me and rubbed his hand soothingly over my back. "He'll be fine. Come on, there's a party and champagne. You'll see, Liam will be back in a few minutes."

Brand was right. We were here for a party, and regardless of my earlier whining, I wasn't a shy wallflower. I soon had a flute of champagne in my hands, and there was a small dance floor that demanded my off-beat attention. I hadn't forgotten about Liam, but I was no longer worried about him.

"Oh my gawd, you're Gil Denver!" A young woman gaped at me. She looked star-struck, but I wasn't a star.

"I am. Why?"

"I loved *Tails from the Urban Jungle*. It's what got me into acting. I can't believe I got to work with Johnny Urban." She clasped her hands to her chest and fluttered her heavy false lashes at me. "Seriously, though. I can't believe my first job was working with Liam James. You're brilliant. They need to make more of your graphic novels into shows. If they ever do *Dating While Single*, please please please let me read for you."

Taken aback, I wasn't sure how to react. *Dating While Single* hadn't even been optioned, but it was flattering to meet someone who was familiar with my work out in the wild.

She rummaged around in a bag hanging across her hips and pulled out a card. Before I could take her card, the party went silent. There was no music, and Benny Skye was trying to get everyone's attention.

"I need everyone looking at me. This is serious, I'm afraid. You're going to hear it a lot over the next few days, but I wanted you to hear this from me first." He held up his phone. "I just got off the phone with Kim Charles. You know her, she worked camera crew. She said she just passed an accident that looked like our Corvette turning into a tumbleweed and cartwheeling across the road. It was bad, real bad. She called to see if that was our car."

I felt the world drop out of my stomach.

The card the actress was trying to hand me fluttered to the floor as she gasped.

Benny took a deep breath before continuing. "Liam was seen driving off in the Corvette about forty minutes ago and has not come back. We don't have confirmation yet, but no one can get a hold of him," Benny Skye continued. "No matter the outcome"— his voice hitched, as if he didn't believe his next words— "*Corvette Summer* is not cursed. And we will release it. We'll do it for Liam."

"For Liam!" it was as if everyone said his name at once, and then everyone and everything fell silent.

I blinked a few times, lost and hopeless, before I found Brand. His face was full of concern as he strode toward me. It wasn't until his arms were around me and I buried my face against his chest that it hit me. I sobbed. Liam had been in that car. I just knew it. I started shaking.

Brand tucked his cheek against my hair and murmured soothing sounds. I heard him sniff. Liam had been important to Brand too. After all, Liam had played Peter in his biography film. He was our friend. And we had been the last people to have seen him alive.

≈

What happened to Liam James?
Find out in the next Second Ending book Bright Phantoms.
Keep reading for a sneak preview.

Get *Bright Phantoms,* now,
or get the box set of the complete series.

EXCERPT FROM BRIGHT PHANTOMS

I had just swung my leg over the rail to the high platform when I heard my name.

I peered down over the edge. It wasn't far, I wasn't the climbing type so it seemed farther away than it really was.

"Yeah, that's me." I called down to the runner who shielded his eyes with a clip board.

"They need you down in makeup."

"What?" That made no sense. I wasn't a makeup artist, and I wasn't an actor. "I don't do makeup, you want Mary." She was the head of special effects makeup and I knew she was on set this week.

"Nope, they sent me after Danica Kensington. Said you

knew about sunscreen." His conversation made less than no sense. "Can you come on down? Glenn requested you specifically."

Oh shit, wonder-kid Glenn Russell was asking for me? Okay he wasn't a kid anymore, he was older than I was, but he came on the scene with a big splash fresh out of UCLA film school, and that reputation clung to him like glitter—there wasn't any easy way to get rid of it.

Well, let it never be said that I left the director of a movie waiting on me for long. I swung my leg back over the side rail and climbed my way down.

"What the hell does Glenn want me for? How the hell does Glenn even know who I am?" I shot off questions a mile a minute as I followed him down and around the path into the ravine where the makeup trailer was parked.

Glenn Russell was at the point of his career where he could write his own paycheck. He hit Hollywood hard with a lightning strike on his first film. Number one box office ticket sales first two weekends, and that was during the Christmas release season. His next film pulled the same magical numbers, but for a total of four weeks and with a June opening. He was movie magic himself when it came to action adventure. Having him on this project was insurance that the studio would have a hit on their hands.

To be honest, the studio was stacking the cards at this point. A *Sebastian Hale Adventure* was a guaranteed hit no matter what. They always earned enough at the box office to ensure there would be more movies made. Then they added to the mix the hottest director of the decade, and let's face it, casting Liam James as Seb Hale was not a dumb move at all. That man was...

I stopped walking. I may have stopped breathing. I don't

get star struck on principal, plus it makes my job really hard to do, but damn.

Liam James stood in front of me, half naked, wearing only his Sebastian Hale requisite loin cloth. Okay, for this particular adventure it was a linen Egyptian kilt. That was part of the story's shtick, no matter where in time Seb Hale ended up, he somehow managed to lose all his modern trappings of civilized clothes. Except for his shoes, and frequently for comedic relief, his sock garters.

I was saved that particular ridiculous look today, he wore proper English riding boots up to his knees. Those were some fine looking knees.

His arms were crossed, and damn if that pose did not make his shoulders look a mile wide and his hips distracting. Kilts shouldn't hang, clinging just below the hip bone like that. It was almost indecent. Not that I was complaining. Liam James was an incredibly good looking man. He had built his career as a blond. But he let the natural dark coloring grow out. I now gazed upon the new Sebastian Hale for the first time, and he stole my breath.

Get Bright Phantoms now to keep reading

Interested in what Gil was writing?
Sign up for Lulu's newsletter to get deleted Johnny Urban scenes
And to keep up to date with new releases and happenings.

Get the deleted scenes and newsletter sign up

∽

Tails from the Urban Jungle is now available!
Start with Book I: The Return of Johnny Urban

ALSO BY LULU M SYLVIAN

Check out these other series

Legatum

Paranormal romantic suspense

The World of Wet Waterfalls

Paranormal reverse harem romance

Rockers

Contemporary Rockstar romance

Holiday Strippers

Contemporary, ridiculous, romance

ABOUT THE AUTHOR

Bio-engineered to be the only redhead in a generation of blonds, Lulu feels that "aliens" may actually be the best answer for a life-time of being asked, "Where did you get that red hair from?"

She did not come into writing from years of scribbling words on paper. Her background is rooted in visual arts and making pictures. Encouraged to make those pictures out of words Lulu began writing just to see what would happen. What happened was two full-length manuscripts in three months.

Lulu cannot ride a horse, a motorcycle, spin a hula hoop, or play roller derby. Yes, she has attempted all of those, even if it has been decades since she's been on a horse or a motorcycle. She embraces the crazy that comes with that one little genetic mutation, and attempts to live up to the reputation that proceeds her. Lulu would like to apologize for her contribution to the hole on the ozone layer from her use of hairspray in the 1980s.

For more information, visit:
www.LuluMSylvian.com

facebook.com/lmsylvian
instagram.com/lmsylvian